for Aziz
Along The Way
toward

A Path With Heart.

R Alan Fuller
October 2010

High Holy Adventure

Shamans, Spirits & Mediums
I Know and Love

By

R Alan Fuller

authorHOUSE

1663 LIBERTY DRIVE, SUITE 200
BLOOMINGTON, INDIANA 47403
(800) 839-8640
www.authorhouse.com

First published by AuthorHouse 10/04/04

ISBN: 1-4184-1694-0 (e)
ISBN: 1-4184-1693-2 (sc)
ISBN: 1-4184-1692-4 (dj)

Library of Congress Control Number: 2004092871

Printed in the United States of America
Bloomington, IN

This book is printed on acid-free paper.

Dedication

This book is dedicated to The Ring, a group of people who have committed themselves to releasing their story and remembering their inherent identity.

Acknowledgements

I state my indebtedness to the dear and many travelers that nobly walked these paths with me at different times and places. Without you there would have been no dance and I am forever grateful for all that you shared. Professors Morton Rosenbaum and Frederic Amory presented literature that reflects our deepest truths. Werner Erhard presented the ecology of mastery. Jack Schwarz demonstrated the human energy systems. F Bruce Lamb shared his wisdon about shamans. Leo Zeff presented illumination beyond understanding. Carlos Castaneda held a line from infinity and showed it to the world. I state my deepest gratitude to each of you for your touch upon my life. Anything worthwhile about this book is due to your encouragement and anything less is solely my responsibility. May The Spirit's blessing always find you. Thank you Victoria Giraud for assistance preparing the manuscript.

From A Course In Miracles™

T-1.II.1. Revelation induces complete but temporary suspension of doubt and fear. 2 It reflects the original form of communication between God and His creations, involving the extremely personal sense of creation sometimes sought in physical relationships. 3 Physical closeness cannot achieve it. 4 Miracles, however, are genuinely interpersonal, and result in true closeness to others. 5 Revelation unites you directly with God. 6 Miracles unite you directly with your brother. 7 Neither emanates from consciousness, but both are experienced there. 8 Consciousness is the state that induces action, though it does not inspire it. 9 You are free to believe what you choose, and what you do attests to what you believe.

T-1.II.2. Revelation is intensely personal and cannot be meaningfully translated. 2 That is why any attempt to describe it in words is impossible. 3 Revelation induces only experience. 4 Miracles, on the other hand, induce action. 5 They are more useful now because of their interpersonal nature. 6 In this phase of learning, working miracles is important because freedom from fear cannot be thrust upon you. 7 Revelation is literally unspeakable because it is an experience of unspeakable love. Awe should be reserved for revelation, to which it is perfectly and correctly applicable.

Preface

My personal experiences with spirits and shamans began in childhood. Although I do not believe I am unique, I had the good fortune to be around adults who did not discount the reality of my "encounters," although not always in a friendly way. Like many children, I saw spirits walking around the house at night, and when I described one in great detail to my grandmother, who lived in the same house, she told me "he" was my grandfather, her husband, who had died years before I was born. That's all she said and offered me no interpretation or comment other than her own honest emotions that told me she missed him, and she didn't. I never doubted what I saw and apparently neither did Grandmother. Except for a single earlier incident, spirits or anything related were never a topic of conversation in my family upbringing.

Between the ages of five and six I lived in a Catholic residential school with several hundred girls. Somehow my mother convinced the nuns to take me in and I was the only boy. One can only wonder at her powers of persuasion to pull that off. Since my fourteen-year-old sister already lived there and my mother did not have the means to care for me and work two jobs at the same time, most likely the nuns meant to offer temporary assistance. I slept on the top floor near the janitor's quarters, away from the girl's dorms. In order to save money my mother had rented a single room in a boarding house where children were not allowed. She had left my father, who was then living in another city at my grandmother's house, where I subsequently lived for five years after this sojourn with the nuns.

I was an insomniac most of my young life, most likely due to stressful circumstances and my own natural biorhythms. Thanks to the nuns, I learned to read at an early age and most nights I would read whatever I could find until I fell asleep. But before I learned to read, at night I would sit in the windowsill of my top-floor room in a multi-story building, which was on a hill that overlooked Kansas City, and remain there into the early morning hours, watching the blinking lights across town. Some nights I would sit sideways in the window and talk to "the kind man with the strange hat and clothes" who walked through the wall and visited with me. Since this was a very traditional Catholic school the message and iconography about Jesus was ubiquitous. In my child's mind I assumed my visitor was the same person the nuns were always teaching us about, the man with the gold hat around his head. I never remembered a lot about what he said to me, but I remember his sweet smell and how much I loved him. It was the only time I felt utterly safe and joyful. In my childlike naiveté, I made the mistake of telling the nuns during one early morning catechism class about my visits with the personage they were teaching us about. The nuns punished me severely enough to bury the memory for many years. I was not punished for lying, but for committing sacrilege. Since I didn't know what that meant, I only knew I had done something very bad and I wasn't supposed to sit in the window.

My father died when I was eleven years old. I was attending a quiet, sedate funeral home service for him, which was filled with somber, reserved people, when suddenly the double doors to the parlor were thrown open. Wailing and sobbing, a group of people quickly rushed in as though they were in a hurry to get there. What a sudden contrast to our sad and quiet traditional service! It shook everyone into full attention as if an explosion had just gone off. These were Native American Indians who had come to pay their last respects. Most of us had no idea my dad had even known them and were totally taken aback. After turning the place upside down with their loud and raucous grief, several enormous men and women picked me up and passionately hugged me while they wailed. A short time later they rushed out as quickly as they had arrived. Instead of being tranquil, the funeral parlor quietness made it impossible for a grief-stricken eleven year old to understand what was real while his life turned inside out once again. Within hours or days, I can't be sure, I had no conscious memory that the Indians had even been there. Not until thirty years later, when I was looking into the face of the Shaman don Eduardo Calderon on a mountain in Peru, did I remember the Indians and my dad.

When I was nine or ten, Dad got me up in the middle of the night and we took a long drive into the rolling cornfields of Kansas from the Missouri side of the river. I did not know where we were going, I only recall enjoying the time with my dad, whom I did not get to see a lot of. After hours of seeing nothing but rolling cornfields, we turned onto a dirt road and approached a large abandoned building that was part of a deserted school. Enough of the auditorium was intact that I could tell it had been the gymnasium. Cars were parked in a haphazard manner all around it, and when we got out of the car I soon noticed we were the only white people there. Strange and wonderful smells from foods I did not recognize came from outside stalls. As we walked toward the gymnasium, we could hear a deep throaty rumbling pounding out of the building. It was so loud and hard that when we opened the doors, the sound almost blew us backwards.

The place was packed and we squeezed along rows of people to find a seat about midway up in the bleachers. They were rickety as we walked on them and shook from the drumming pounding from the floor. I don't recall why they were drumming or having had much interest at that point, but probably like any youngster, I eventually left the bleachers to explore. I ended up in the stairwell and ran into about a half-dozen kids who were all red-skinned Indians and I was white, a fact that aroused their ire. There were too many of them for me to get away and I was getting beaten up pretty badly when suddenly these enormous hands lifted two boys off my chest who were pounding my face, and then they all ran off. A tall burly Indian man looked at me without a drop of pity. He simply picked me up off the floor as he pulled a handkerchief from his pocket and wiped blood from my nose, then gently rubbed my back and walked on.

Very much in a daze, both from the beating I had just received and the ear- shattering drumming that caused every part of the dilapidated wooden floors to shake, I no longer knew where I was. I opened a door and found myself on the dance floor where dozens of warriors were performing an ecstatic trance dance; rattlesnakes hung from their necks and arms while they spun and leaped and whirled. Many more snakes coiled and hissed around the floor. I was a Tom Sawyer kind of kid from St. Joe, Missouri, and my many treks to the swamps along the river had made me familiar with rattlesnakes. I was normally afraid of them and I knew not to get close, but I remember looking at this entire scene without any emotion, simply witnessing what was before me, perhaps incapable of understanding.

In a complete daze, most likely a trance, I walked out into the middle of the dance floor while legs and bodies whizzed past me from the dancers, who moved like intoxicated gymnasts. Dressed in full Indian regalia with chiseled powerful bodies, the dancers made thunderous moves at the speed of football players running a sweep. I had no reaction to any of it as I stood in front of a hissing water moccasin at my feet. No one on the dance floor was even aware of my presence. They were so deep in trance—eyes rolled back into their heads—that they had no way of noticing me. Had any of them hit me, I would have been easily knocked down and likely not even noticed. Suddenly a very ancient, white-haired man sitting next to the drummers at the edge of the dance floor commanded my attention with his eyes, which radiated like a lighthouse beacon pulling me toward him with irresistible allure. I walked toward his eyes in a straight line across the mayhem in movement on the dance floor. Not once did a dancer, except for some feathers and stinging tassels, ever hit me and no snakes bit me though I stepped over many.

I stood in front of this ancient man, but he remained seated and gave no overt response to me other than through his eyes. I had no way of realizing at the time that he was the officiating shaman of this ceremony, but even at such a tender age I somehow grasped he was no ordinary person. To this day I remember his eyes shining like a radiant crystal from an otherwise implacable and wizened face. Without words, he told me that I should remain with him for a while but no doubt my dad refused the offer. I never remembered any of this experience after my dad's funeral until Shaman Don Eduardo pulled it out of my eyes.

Very soon after first meeting don Eduardo, he insisted I had a mark on my eyes that had been placed there by a shaman and he wanted to know about this shaman. At first I was confused and did not understand what he was talking about. I held his stare, however, and then it all came back to me, flooding my thoughts with lucid images, visceral feelings and even tastes and smells, such as the tobacco and incense in the auditorium and the food cooked near the cars. Only then did I remember that incident on the dance floor with the snake-dancing Indians and realize why shamans had such an attraction in my life. I never did learn any details of what might have been my dad's connection with Midwest Indians around Kansas in the '50's. Dad owned a café and tavern on "the rough side of town" and my aunt believed he fed and took care of some Indian families from that side of town when they were down on their luck. Unfortunately, by the time I remembered these childhood experiences there was no one alive in my family of origin to ask for any details.

My tales are a highly focused selection from my personal experiences with shamans, spirits and mediums I know and love. Some have passed but many are still among us. It will take at least two more books to complete my tales and I hope to accomplish this goal. While writing about memories is never the same as what occurred, to the limits of my writing ability I have told exactly what happened. I changed the identities of the travelers where it was unclear if they would appreciate being recognized or if I had no way of asking. The shamans, mediums and spirits are all real and called by their own names.

Over the years I have told my closest friends some of these stories, but I have made very little effort until now to share them with the world. Some say I owe this record to my generation. I don't know if I do or not but publishing these tales begin my contribution to our collective record and hopefully our appreciation for these sacred paths too often neglected, exaggerated or marginalized in our common understanding. Even though I am being candid and literal, it does not mean anything I write is The Truth, however, and I make no such inference. But it is the best I am able to describe. There are not very many people who have actually walked these paths. Those who write "about" such things offer a different record than those who were there.

In love and light,

R Alan Fuller
Nevada City, California

CHAPTER ONE

Initiation Journey
with Shaman
don Eduardo Calderon

In Peru many years ago I was part of a group of twenty-four, participating in an exotic series of initiations being orchestrated and delivered by one of the most extraordinary shamans of our times. Never before or since have I traveled with a bolder group of serious spiritual practitioners. Most of us had made trips to Peru before, specifically to work directly with an indigenous shaman to learn his craft, which meant being accepted by someone capable of delivering such training. This trip was very different than taking a vacation to be around a shaman or to experience one of their ceremonies. We were a group already dedicated to the path of the shaman, and because we had become known in different shamanic circles around the world, we were invited to participate in this rare opportunity.

Shamans are masters of the ecstatic trance and whatever means they employ to get there, and in that capacity they can function as communication intermediaries between exalted realms normally outside the purview of our consciousness. They are not priests or religious representatives, and shamanism is not a religion. Real shamans have inherited sophisticated primeval practices originating from prehistory that are methods field-tested by countless generations to establish energetic links between our everyday experience and the invisible realm of the spirit. In this sense most especially, shamans exist as a living bridge between the realm of the invisible and the practical spiritual needs of the community they serve. From the exotic realms they travel within their ecstasies, shamans bring useful information and energetic effects to guide, to heal and to assist our day-to-day living as well as to serve our spiritual illumination.

Shamans also practice worldly occupations: a shaman might be a furniture maker, a healer charging for his/her services, or most any other occupation. A shaman is always a shaman and their inherent traits are available to them always, but they do not always interact in a shaman capacity with the world. Don Eduardo told me that in ancient Peruvian civilizations such as the Incas, it was mandatory that the shamans also practice a craft or a profession for a living. Indigenous traditions say that the average person has no way to assess the quality and caliber of a shaman's spiritual reality and that could pose inordinate risks to the people who rely on their services. Watch what they do in the world, observe how they operate within their profession or craft, the ancients tell us. Do they make great furniture, charge a fair price, and treat customers well? Do you feel good when you use their furniture at home? A shaman cannot help but place their mood, their touch, the level at which they conceptualize the world into their work, so look there for signposts, the ancients say.

Among this group of travelers, most practiced shamanism within the fabric of their lives and brought enough experience to make our journey extraordinary. Beyond that we had not much in common and even our practices varied widely. Some in the group relished daily exotic ceremonies such as: greeting the morning sun, praying to the *apus* or the spirit presence of the mountains, praying to *Wankan Tanka* or the sky father God of the Central Plains Indians, or praying to *Pacha Mama* or the earth mother goddess of the Incas. Some even prayed to the Christian saints, others revered the Buddha and some of us participated in all of it! Others kept their prayers internal and without display, other than during ceremony. Many dressed colorfully in ceremonial regalia while others preferred simple camp clothing. The pressure we produced on each other pushed many of us beyond our

2

limitations and would prove positive and challenging, causing me to investigate my experience for many years.

The final leg of our initiation journey, following five days in the high country wilderness beyond Machu Pichu, was a two-day trek to the infamous Marcawasi Lagoons, an ancient sorcerer's lair where indigenous sorcerers had been initiated since before the Incas. According to these ancient traditions, a sorcerer is a shaman gone bad, corrupted by power and lust for personal gain, the exact opposite of the shaman who is dedicated to the health and well-being of the community and formally makes his or herself available on that basis. I daresay if the sorcerers could be heard, they would offer a different description of their path and whom they are, but that's what the shamans have to say about it.

I once asked don Eduardo, half-joking but also serious, if a group of shamans gets together and takes a vote on who has become a sorcerer? I thought I was being facetious but I was also trying to understand how a person attains the title of "sorcerer" in the Peruvian world with its unique ancestral heritage. To my surprise but typical of his very different thought patterns, he responded that shamans do indeed get together and decide on who is a sorcerer, but only after the shaman in question had already somehow declared himself to be a sorcerer. Among other things, that meant a kind of personal marketing and advertising, alerting the world that he or she could be approached on that basis. For example, both a shaman and a sorcerer might be approached to help a distraught marriage partner whose mate was having an affair. According to don Eduardo, it would have been understood and expected that the shaman would try to heal or fix the problem for the cuckolded partner by improving the marriage. A sorcerer, on the other hand, would accept payment to help the emotionally injured partner to reap their revenge and would be approached on that basis. These opposite ways of using power have been prevalent in South America for probably thousands of years. The personal power of both the shaman and the sorcerer determines

3

the nature of the requests they can accept as well as the remedy they can deliver.

Don Eduardo made a clear distinction between the shaman and the sorcerer and it was fairly black and white in his mind. The sorcerer used his power to control, dominate or manipulate people for personal gain, while the shaman drew on the *power* of the medicine wheel to heal, to help, and above all to continually make contact with the invisible realms to affirm our spiritual identity. In practice, however, these distinctions were far from simple, along with most everything else in the world of Peruvian shamans. The Marcawasi Lagoons is a sorcerer's lair and going to such a power spot was an initiation for would-be adepts needing to learn about such distinctions.

Our final campsite was at 17,000 feet and for five days we enacted ancient shamanic ceremonies repeated by countless generations to make our bid for a rightful place among the energies and spirits that inhabit that otherworldly landscape. We had come from Europe, North and South America, Africa and Asia, each of us for a single purpose, to be initiated by Shaman don Eduardo Calderon of Trujillo, Peru, as a shaman of his lineage. Throughout the world don Eduardo was known as the Wizard of the Four Winds; he is a shaman master who can invoke the *power* of the four directions of the medicine wheel to do all the things shamans are reputed to do. My tale will reveal what that means since it cannot be easily explained any more than one can explain a kiss.

Don Eduardo had declared some years earlier that his visions had shown him that "the new shamans would come from the West," and we had come to fulfill his vision. Don Eduardo was the first well-known, fully-recognized shaman to ever make that declaration or to offer to train Westerners on that basis. There was no guarantee that anyone would be initiated as a shaman with his blessing, and unfortunately some took that to mean they had to compete as if such an identity could be won over others. Most of us recognized we could help or hinder each other's progress but no one except the shaman, Spirit, and our personal determination could decide our fate. Our group was composed of every kind of character for a play filled with high drama. Don Eduardo had foretold that *power,* the shaman's concept for intentionally deployed spiritual energy, and *mescalito,* the shaman's inter-dimensional *ally,* would make it clear when and who was to be initiated. That meant visions and non-ordinary reality entered into with the shaman would be the final arbiter. I never conceived it could be any other way, but it was far from simple.

By the time we reached the mountaintop, our journey was teeming with personal dramas of all kinds, and the play had swelled to such proportions that no one could turn around even if they had wanted to. There was no cavalry to save us if anything went wrong, and practically speaking, it was a day's hike to a distant mountain village. Occasionally, powerful men and sometimes even the women challenged each other for authority and control; some made moves to dominate anyone too weak to resist. More than a few looked to me to lead our group when Shaman don Eduardo refused to deal with us collectively except during ceremony, which meant it was entirely up to us in what emotional condition we arrived at the circle when he called.

At first I was single-mindedly focused on my own process and not paying much attention to what anyone thought about me, both a strength and weakness. By the time I realized that others were looking to me to offer some leadership, it was too late for me to remain in the background, unseen by the alpha male who sought that position. Big Beau had been a warrior in military special services and a self-declared patriot who ran a wilderness tracking school, and was one of the most daringly dominating men I have ever been around. The pressure he placed on everyone to "submit" to his dominance was an extraordinary gift, though few saw it that way at the time. I remember him with gratitude. Eventually we would run out of food before we completed the initiations and when the temperature dropped to 10 degrees, our responsibilities included keeping several people alive in their tents while the rest of us continued. We would all see it through to the end and for some of us it would lead to an extraordinary new beginning.

CHAPTER TWO

Marcawasi: An Otherworldly Bowl

Sunrise came early as I peered out the little screen window of my tent the first morning at Marcawasi. Gigantic walls with vertical serpentine ridges and escarpments jutting like flying buttresses from gothic cathedrals rose hundreds of feet all around. We were camped on a rocky level surface the size of a sports arena playing field. One could easily envision an ancient rocket ship landing there, one of several legends about this place, with its jets burning down into the mountain, leaving this unnatural bowl we camped in. I have hiked in many kinds of mountainous terrain but nothing I had ever seen could compare to this place. Inexplicable black appeared like gigantic drapes hanging from the huge vertical walls, which reinforced the mystique that a powerful heat burnt this enormous hole into the mountain. From the floor looking up, the mountain appeared to climax at the top edges of the bowl. After hiking an almost indiscernible path to the tops of the cliffs, it was a surprise to find myself looking over a vast rolling landscape that gave off an ancient feeling as if the wildness were inhabited. Later I would discover the vast mountain was punctuated with the debris of unknown ancient civilizations.

On our second day Shaman don Eduardo instructed us to go and meditate in the surrounding countryside but to remain vigilant and not to allow anything to sneak up on us. We were to select a meditation site and then to create a circle of stones around us for energetic protection. This simple practice, when conscientiously performed in a highly intentional manner in a wilderness environment, has a definite and serious effect. It can be akin to circling up the wagons and declaring your boundaries that you will protect with your life as well as an inner-generated,

7

psychically textured lattice of light and love. The circle of stones becomes a personal power spot to face the wilderness engulfing you.

I had heard this kind of instruction many times before when we would be out for a long time, but this meditation was only supposed to be for a few hours to prepare ourselves for the evening's fire ceremony. There was an element of genuine concern in don Eduardo's voice that I had never heard before. He had always been matter-of-fact or entirely confident when dealing with incorporeal life forms, and I had come to trust in his ability to deal with virtually anything otherworldly. Don Eduardo said the only time a shaman goes to Marcawasi is to claim his/her standing among the ancient sorcerers. He said at one time these sorcerers were shamans before they became seduced to follow a darker path of power than the goals of the shaman. When he first started talking about Marcawasi months earlier, at first I thought he meant actual people lived there. Eventually I realized he was talking about "real entities who still lived there," only they no longer had physical bodies.

Don Eduardo claimed the old sorcerers' energies that dwelled in this powerful place would try to overcome our spirits and make us into one of them. This shaman initiation included making these rogue spirits acknowledge each of us as a shaman and not sorcerers like they had become, something he told us was extremely difficult to accomplish. Succeeding in this initiation meant action, making something occur, and not merely relying on internal meditative insights. As bizarre as it sounds, don Eduardo meant what he said, but none of us could know what he was talking about before experiencing it. How could spirit sorcerers, without physical bodies, give us their blessing as a shaman, acknowledging we were not one of them? It was a total mind twist to my thinking. It was so circular and self-referencing a proposition that all I could do was accept it or reject it, but I could not argue with it.

It was not until the following day that I understood some of his concern. I did not venture very far from the bowl since virtually any place one selected on that mountain mesa of rolling stone dotted with pockets of lagoons had a breathtaking panoramic view. Hiking was not my priority this day though I was absorbed by the majesty and eeriness of the environs. I quickly found a spot and dropped into a very quiet and long meditation. I wanted and needed to be ready for this evening's ceremony. What was to happen that night was the event we had all been waiting and preparing for throughout our weeks of travel. During the upcoming fire ceremony we would present ourselves before the Wizard of the Four Winds and he would decide whether we would be initiated as a shaman. At least that is what we expected!

A Cast of Characters

Before nightfall there was a great deal more interpersonal play among the cast of characters on this trip.

"Fuller! I need a readiness assessment from you NOW!" commanded Big Beau, his powerful voice projecting from over my shoulder and pulling me away from a conversation with several others from our group. By giving me a direct order in front of others, Big Beau had decided to test me before the fire ceremony to see how I would respond. "I need to alert don Eduardo if anyone has crapped out," Beau asserted, as though grave importance hung in the balance and I needed to jump to attention.

I turned around, not surprised to see Big Beau standing so close I could see he enjoyed peering downwards to meet my line of sight. "I've taken care of it, Beau," I replied, "so what do you want to know?"

"I want a face-to-face check-in and not your opinion," Beau demanded as though he rejected my words while enjoying the moment to press his case. "Get me a count of who's ready and who's not," he ordered, "and I need it NOW!"

"I've just completed rounds with everyone except you," I replied dryly.

"Tell don Eduardo everyone is ready," I added with a fake friendly smile, "unless you're not planning on attending. Otherwise, everyone is strong and ready to go."

For a moment Big Beau tensed as his muscles flexed and his posture leaned into me. His lip started to rise with yet another escalating demand. Then the thought hit him about what I had said and he stood taut for a few moments, processing what he wanted to do. "You spoke directly to everyone?" Beau tested me one more time with his question.

"Everyone is ready," I said without answering him directly.

My reply sidestepped compliance or defiance, which eventually Big Beau managed to perturb in most everyone. Instead, I presented him with a moment he had not anticipated. I stood looking him in the eye while my body involuntarily and subtly postured to fight, but mentally I was intending just the opposite. I knew this was not my moment to deal with Beau; the very last thing I wanted was a confrontation with this complex and amazing man, a dark force in my book on the one hand, while also being one of the most unique travelers I had ever shared a fire ceremony with. And I have been to the fire with more than a few profound beings who fully deserve that description.

As a shaman initiate on this journey, Beau deserved my respect, and I sincerely took any opportunity that presented itself to let him know that without ever acquiescing to his litany of instructions and demands. I believed at that time that only a trained fighter could defeat me, so I was not generally afraid of aggressive men, but Big Beau was that very kind of person I did not want to tangle with. Yet I knew I would have to settle something with him or what I came for would not happen. He had already tested one man to the limit, one of the most impressive displays of controlled power I had ever witnessed.

Machu Pichu High Country a Week Before Marcawasi

About a week or so earlier we were on the third and last day of walking the switchbacks of the Inca trail, entire days of hiking up and up, eventually reaching a beautiful saddle peak at 14,500 elevation. When we arrived five days later at the outback temple behind Machu Pichu, don Eduardo was already waiting for us. He would escort us into the sacred city at midnight. One of the shamans scheduled to lead the hike had left for a family emergency, so he entrusted Big Beau, with his mountain tracking school experience, to lead the hiking logistics of the journey, even though we had experienced guides taking care of us and more than twenty porters. The porters were necessary because at that time in Peru guerilla warfare was rampant in the countryside and a very large group could easily and quickly disappear in those vast mountains of the high Andes. A large contingent of local Indians in their brilliant ponchos, carrying everything needed for camp, was a picturesque site on the trail but also a practical matter. We hoped their colors would signal only a friendly presence. We also required their support so we would have time and energy for ceremony, rather than having to deal with the necessities of backpacking camp life.

There was no doubt about it: Big Beau was a powerful mountain man in every respect, six foot five of rippling muscles, strappingly handsome and skilled at navigating wilderness terrain. Most of all he was amazing to watch: many times every day he would make moves with people that no one I had ever been around would dream of. Most of the time he treated most of us as though he was the general and everyone else was a part of the troops. He was so natural and dominating about it that he got away with it. Even more amazing, many of the group totally bought into his domination because it was easier, or seemed so at first. Eventually he was telling us where or whether to fill our canteens, where to set up our latrines, and much more. Beau gave new meaning to the idea of bending over when told, and some literally did!

R Alan Fuller

The second day in the outback I had watched him order the youngest woman on the journey to take a walk with him giving the impression that urgent business needed immediate attention. Michelle was mid to late twenties and overly confidant, a writer who had wangled her place on the journey as an observer/writer. She was a very pleasant trail companion with a positive outlook and she wanted to write a book about shamans more than become a shaman and in this sense she was not entirely on a par with everyone else. Still I enjoyed her presence among us, and she would frequently surprise me with her strong participation. She was in superb physical condition, and her interest in shamanism was sincere, but in my opinion she had little clue what she had gotten herself into which initially caused me to feel somewhat protective toward her. To my surprise, she immediately went with Big Beau, looking at first reserved and then compliant at Beau's insistence. Partly out of curiosity and partly out of concern, I snuck off after them by hiking around the hillside from the other direction. I was not exactly sure I would even find them since it was a substantial walk through thick vegetation taller than me and I was concerned I might get lost.

In about a half-hour I came around a rocky bend dripping lianas in every direction that served me as handholds. I stepped around a rock ledge with a forest outcrop above it and a totally unexpected sight came into view. While my perch remained completely hidden, I could see them standing in the clearing ahead of me and slightly downhill. At first I was utterly stunned by what I saw, then amazed, and then a little confused about how I felt. I immediately became fascinated and aroused, emotions that contrasted with a flimsy dose of self-righteous judgment, which tried to mask a disturbing jealousy. These two were more than enjoying themselves and required nothing from me.

I was transfixed, transported, and sent to heaven and hell with my feelings all over the board as I stepped back into the thick lianas. Many times the unexpected had frozen me in my tracks on a jungle path though nothing could have prepared me for such an

12

encounter. Thank you, Michelle and Beau. I silently bowed with genuine appreciation and walked back to camp. Every kinky Greek myth and the endless fornication tales that imbue spiritual and religious literature from The Old Testament to the Incas had just earned a newfound authenticity in my practical understanding.

At the end of the journey, when she was heartbroken because Beau had no further interest in her, I told Michelle I had unexpectedly seen them that afternoon in the mountains. I asked her what had motivated her to go with Beau in the first place and that I sincerely wanted to understand her attraction to someone so obvious about his agendas. To my surprise, she said she had no idea why she went with Beau and although I accepted her statement I was not entirely convinced.

Nobody argued much with his barking orders about this and that. Sometimes it was humorous in a way we all enjoyed, but became less and less so as time went by. We all kind of tolerated his habit of heading out in front with the guides and then dropping back to tell us what the next few hours would be like, as if we were eager to hear his report. He was constantly animated, bold and more than outgoing, obviously in elements he felt comfortable in, and he appeared to care less how he affected anyone except that they comply. Gradually he became increasingly demanding, telling people how to pack, how to hike, and not trying to veil his real agenda, that he was the king kahuna on this trip. Truthfully, he displayed a lot of craft and talent in more dimensions than I initially gave him credit for. In his own way, at times he was truly stupendous among a crowd who themselves were masters and adepts of many kinds in their own right. This was no group of ordinary folks. In fact, there were some very advanced spiritual adepts on this journey: one world renowned Zen master, a Caucasian couple from a Native American tribe who were widely recognized, a master Chinese herbalist, two advanced martial artists, three doctors, a lawyer, a film producer, wealthy inheritors and international businessmen and women. All were very experienced in one way or another.

Not surprisingly, at least to me, the Zen master never let Beau's behavior affect him. He was also the one person Big Beau never bothered and occasionally deferred to. The Caucasian Native American trained couple, on the other hand, was constantly outraged and critical of not only Beau's behavior, but also everyone else's at one time or another. This couple's complaints were mostly hilarious because they never had an answer for just exactly "who" was the person to whom to address their endless complaints. *Who was responsible for whom?* Most of us recognized that very question went to the heart of our drama that was no doubt a part of don Eduardo's designs to ready us for initiation. In the more intellectually sophisticated circles of shamanism it's called *cognitive dissonance*, situations that force us out of ordinary thinking and patterned ways of perceiving the world around us. An accident or an unexpected crisis, for example, takes most of us beyond our normal awareness and in those moments we are filled with altered perceptions and elevated sensibilities. The task for the shaman is to produce as much cognitive dissonance as possible without shattering the ability to respond in a purposeful manner. In this case, all don Eduardo had to do was leave us to our own devices on the way to his initiations.

At one point this couple's complaints reached such a comical crescendo, at least in the eyes of some of the more deranged minds on this journey, that late one night the Zen Roshi and I got to laughing so hard that we almost passed out. We had forgotten about the thin air. I got really dizzy and a little nauseated because we were joking about Beau being everyone's spiritual benefactor and the white couple, who dressed sometimes like Indians in the movies, did not seem to realize that they looked as strange to us sometimes as we to them. We laughed mostly at ourselves, and the Roshi was merciless. In his own way, long before I saw it, he could have kissed Beau from sheer gratitude for the self-illuminating opportunities he presented us. The perfect cast of characters!

One of the women on this trip, one of two who had electrified us walking the lagoon, an initiation I will relate, was very much an authentic candidate for initiation by don Eduardo. She was an utterly serious shaman whose boldness could be beyond belief, though her spiritual reality was not yet fully formed. Not only was Lorena not intimidated by Big Beau, she was his match and then some at every turn. I thought she had made a mistake at the time, and years later, drinking my best cabernet late one night, I told her so. We laughed and she enjoyed my opinion but she still didn't agree. When Beau made his move on her the third night on the trail, at an ancient Inca ruin where we had camped, she immediately turned the tables on him and escorted him into the bushes where she proceeded to fuck his brains out, so to speak. I guess that was Lorena's way of letting Beau know who was in charge.

Listening to those two, obviously not as far away as they had thought they were, was a lesson in energy that put everyone on notice, regardless of our personal reactions. The sounds were outlandish, evoking images of satyrs trysting in the forest nearby. I think it was Harmon, a film producer, who joked that he would make a fortune if he had documented it on tape. The energy and boldness on this journey was off the charts! Lorena and I and Big Beau would have a final showdown at the initiation fire ceremony at Marcawasi ten days later.

Kamala was another strong feminine presence on our journey and the other woman to flawlessly walk the lagoon. She was married to Harmon, who was a quiet and dignified man. About thirty-five years old, Kamala was elegance wrapped in beauty and grace and going on age seventy in wisdom. She moved around the camp like one of King Solomon's priestesses, utterly authentic and serene, literally exotic in every respect and with zero pretension about anything. She had an athletic physique like a belly dancer and her movements frequently reminded me of Middle Eastern dance. No matter how bone tired and wasted after a grueling day of hiking, she had a bright scarf in her lapel and her camping clothes still looked fresh. When Kamala visited with us around the camp, she would always be telling us something that went straight to the heart. She and Harmon were senior students of Karlfreid Von Durkheim, a famous European mystic who wrote *The Way of Transformation* and lived in the Black Forest outside of Vienna at his spiritual community. I had studied his book and his writing had deeply affected me to the point of major life changes. I had no idea he had a spiritual community, so it was an equal treat to meet some of his students, who were everything I would expect in people dedicated to his teachings.

How fascinating it is for me to look back and realize that Harmon at the time looked something like I do now, and similar in age. He was then in his early 50's, thin in hair and body, reserved and completely distinct from his exotic wife, except for a gleam in his eyes that matched hers. His power was very quiet, though awesome, as I was soon to discover. Their utterly beautiful "coupleness" left not the slightest doubt they were entirely connected to each other, even though they did not behave like most couples. Harmon was never bothered in the slightest when Kamala visited with others, no matter what time or how she did it. He knew she clearly reserved her expressed affections for him alone, and they were obviously secure in each other's love.

The second evening in camp Big Beau said something off the wall to Kamala as she walked by him, returning from the brush where we all eventually headed for personal needs. Typical of Beau there was no preamble. "You're attracting the mountain jaguars with your period blood," Beau solemnly said as he stepped toward Kamala.

It was difficult to tell whether he was trying to be seductive or if he was going to tell her what to do with her tampons, or something even more personal. Before he could launch his next sentence, Kamala projected her voice like a Shakespearean stage actress strolling across the set. "Your shamanic command of the lower regions is truly inspiring, Beau," Kamala replied without losing stride. "But I'm sure the jaguars can take care of themselves and don't need your worry."

Her reply stopped him in his tracks and everyone knew it was complete between them. Not even Big Beau would risk crossing intellects with her again. To his credit (or dementia) I have to hand it to Big Beau: not only was he not dissuaded, he eventually made a direct move on every woman on the journey, each in a unique way but always to establish his dominance or control. Eventually he cornered, forced, seduced or cowered a response from most everyone in the group with a few exceptions. He appeared completely impervious to what anyone thought while remaining actively engaged with as many as would accept enrollment into whatever he was about at the time.

We had twenty-five porters carrying everything except our personal daypacks. We could be strewn out over a mile or more by the time we came into camp. It was the job of the porters (Indians from the high country who truly "served" what we were doing) to have camp set up with hot tea waiting when we arrived for lunch and dinner. The porters had two trail bosses, one a guide we worked with regularly, and the other a local from a nearby village. Both men were experienced mountaineers and were always out in front of everyone during the arduous walks. Because of the altitude, the hearts of the native Indians who live in the Andes are twice the physical size and capacity of most everyone else on the planet. Walking these mountains was the only world these men had ever known. Always wrapped in their ponchos, they carried loads by first placing a blanket on the ground, piling everything onto it, then tying the ends securely with a foursquare knot and then heaving it onto their shoulders. In order to balance the load, they had to lean forward while holding the knot ends. Wearing rough sandals and pajama style tops and bottoms, the porters probably resembled those who walked this same trail a thousand years earlier. It was a great five-day income for the porters, more than they made from months of farming or picking coca leaves, but still a hard job at times and they earned their worth. They literally had to run ahead of our group after meal preparation and kitchen cleanup in order to have camp ready for us when we arrived.

This arrangement not only provided an exotic amenity to our travel but also safety and necessity. The porters were native to the mountains, while for us the walking was physically demanding, no matter what our conditioning. If we had not assigned one of the porters to carry a set of oxygen bottles, I think at least one fatality would have occurred in our group. Even I got altitude sickness one night and in those conditions it would have been life threatening if the temperature dropped. I had been dry heaving for hours while sweating so heavily that my sleeping bag had become drenched. I knew I was in serious trouble and still could not stop the chronic gag reflex that was sapping my strength. Late in the night several people came to my tent and helped me to change into dry clothing while holding me from behind and placing pressure on my solar plexus while insisting I chew some cocoa leaves. It worked. Dry and breathing right, no longer gagging, I could sip water to rehydrate and by morning I felt OK. I was the last hold out to chew the cocoa leaves and never made that mistake again.

So we looked out for each other very carefully in this regard and everyone learned the profound and invisible power of chewing coca leaves when hiking high altitudes. We could breathe better and consequently feel better when we kept a little wad of the green leaf in our cheeks. We had quickly adapted to the local custom among guides, porters and pilgrims. Even Big Beau by the second day was lecturing us on how to properly mix the necessary ash in the chew to get the desired effect. We all had our little handful of green leaves the size of rose petals bought for fifty cents at the train station where we had disembarked to head for the trailhead. Everyone knew about the beneficial effects of coca leaves.

Virtually every traveler who arrives at a hotel in Cuzco is immediately served *coca de mate* tea, which is simply brewed coca leaves. Without the coca, it would be extremely difficult to adjust coming from the Lima airport, which is at sea level, to Cuzco, which is at 11,000 feet elevation, in about an hour. Unlike the notorious cocaine that is derived from coca leaves, chewing the leaves or sipping the tea has no narcotic effect whatsoever. In fact, you never feel anything except being able to breathe better, which in turn affects how strongly you can move. If you don't drink the tea in the first couple of hours, most people will get altitude sickness. When it comes to exertion at high altitudes there simply is no substitute.

Because there were practical reasons to maintain a strict separation, we maintained a certain respect regarding the porters by only communicating with our lead guides when on the trail. Most of the porters only spoke Quechua and it could sometimes be heartbreaking to watch the trail bosses handle the discipline and regimentation necessary to do their work. It was easier on them and on us to stay out of it.

For example, one time when I had gotten out in front of our group and accidentally caught up with the porters, I approached them while they were taking a trailside break for lunch. The trail boss was screaming at them for their slow pace and threatening to deduct the pay of anyone who did not keep up. Then he held up two Western-looking packages of white bread and threw them down onto the trail. In an instant there was a stampede that looked like ponchos, sandal heels and diving bodies all heading for the same targets. Within seconds, after a few fights for possession, half the hands, maybe less, came up with a slice of bread. If they wanted dinner, the trail boss commanded, already walking ahead and signaling them to head out, they would have to keep his pace. I saw the pain and anguish in the eyes of younger, older and slighter men who did not have the strength or the position to grab their piece of bread and I had to turn away and walk back down the trail. I believe none met my eyes and I was grateful for that. No matter what it looked like to me, I did my best not to judge it and my respect for these mountain Indians to know how to conduct their own affairs was genuine. But it did bother me.

I did break the rule later that day, however, by offering some trail mix to a teenager struggling with his load and walking with a limp, miles behind the rest of the porters. We were all alone as I rapidly walked up behind him and his painfully slow pace.

The path was a six-foot-wide stone path weaving through a bog that was filled with knee and waist-high muddy water and thick vegetation. At first he didn't know if he should accept my offer but his hunger overcame him. Having seen how the trail bosses managed their crew, I felt cautious, not wanting to do the wrong thing and get him in trouble. I got him to take a couple of aspirin, rubbed a menthol balm on his temples and knees, gave him some of my coca leaves that he gratefully accepted, and convinced him to let me carry his load for awhile. I kept joking that I wanted to feel the weight, doing so in pantomime since we spoke nothing in common. It worked and about an hour later I returned his load and walked on ahead of him and we never spoke again.

This particular day I had delighted in racing the lead guide to one of the vistas, to everyone's amazement, most especially my own. We had been traveling a half-day with the sun popping in and out of the clouds and temperature swings of 15 and 20 degrees within a few minutes. We had to manage our body temperature by constantly zipping our jackets open and closed. Awed by the surroundings, by who we were and what we were doing, I had been gradually falling more and more into a trance, and it all began to well up in me. It just felt plain awesomely good to be there, and each step was more and more energizing. I began to visualize, from a deep inner place, the power animals of the medicine wheel: the horse and the dragon. I was not trying to envision anything so much as it was just happening. Increasingly, I was filling with energy and I began to jog without really thinking about how it felt so good to move like that. Increasingly, bursts of energy and enormous joy ran up my spine like a wind inflating me. Then a burst of energy ran into me as if the energy animals and I were the same entity. Straight up the mountain I ran feeling the Dragon of the North rushing through me. The metaphor became reality, the *gait of power* as it is sometimes called in shamanism. It was one of the most glorious experiences of my life, a run up a world-class switchback trail riding the tail of the dragon to 14,500 feet.

True to form, one of the lead guides beat me to the top by fifty yards. When I began jogging he was a mile or more ahead on the steep switchbacks. Due to the steepness of the trail we could mostly see each other up or down the pass. The guide no doubt heard me coming up the trail from the whoops and hollers my companions sent after me, floating echoes up the V shape mountain pass that only added to my joy. While running in this glorious state of strength and well-being, without meaning to I not only ran past the lead local Indian, but also past Big Beau, who had always felt triumphant by being the first white guy to the top. He tried but could not keep up with me as I landed on the saddle peak with the lead guide laughing and embracing me as I arrived. He quickly offered me one of his Peruvian cigarettes, appreciating it was a rare treat to find a Westerner keeping up with him as well as enjoying his smoke breaks. I fully realize that most of us think that tobacco and physically hardy health are contradictions, but it was a rare mountain guide who did not take smoke breaks and no one can argue with their robust health. Including me in his tobacco ritual was the icing on the cake after a strong push up a leg of the mountain. We sat on a comfortable rock and slid our packs off while we enjoyed our tobacco. We looked down from our ridge perch atop the mountainside watching our companions as they dotted the trail in the distance, moving steadily upward, some looking like distant dark spots among the vistas. It would be a couple of hours before everyone made it to the top.

About ten minutes after me, Big Beau walked onto the high ground and our eyes met for a moment. To his credit, I believe he understood me and displayed his respect with a slight nod of the head that I did not miss when he came onto the high ground. He was sometimes contemptuous when anyone smoked cigarettes, admonishing them that they would not have enough wind power for the high country, although somehow the ceremonial pipe was acceptable to his standards and he smoked in the evenings with the rest of us. I admit I enjoyed putting it in his face that cigarettes or not, there was no way he was ever going to walk me into the ground in these mountains.

A short while later several men were within a hundred yards of the top. Beau took his pack off and walked over to the center of the trailhead and started yelling. "What kind of pace is thattt...?" shouted this military drill instructor voice, which pushed down the trail like a harsh burst of wind.

Beau had his hands cupped to the side of his mouth like a bullhorn and he was nervously moving sideways, back and forth as he yelled. "Which is ittt, your pack's too tight or too loose? 'Cause they must be holding up your pace. Tight'n it up, or loosen 'em but get it in gear." Beau was really getting animated and raising the decibels shooting down the pass. "You look like your power animal is Bambi! I don't see any jaguars down there, it looks like Bambi on a stroll."

It must have been the altitude because that one got me laughing, but it was getting very uncomfortable while Beau got more and more intense.

"What makes you think you're shaman material if you can't even glide up a simple hike? I'm not gonna be late for Eduardo in Machu Pichu if you can't keep uppp," his voice burst down into that vast space. "Where's your warrior spirit?" On and on he went. He was relentless like a drill sergeant in boot camp.

Wow! This guy is from another planet, I thought to myself. I honestly could not tell if Big Beau was psychotic, a master of play, or both, but it was producing an edge that no one had dreamed of having to deal with, especially on a spiritual journey. The two martial artists on the journey were fuming and at times completely flabbergasted like the rest of us. I could see their mounting tension and incredulity that this person even existed, let alone was in our midst and not going away. Did he really mean to bust our chops if we didn't follow his program, and whether he did or didn't, what was the proper behavior called for here? Clearly, fighting would be utterly disgraceful, but equally uncomfortable was the patent failure to maintain personal presence with dignity and strength.

The tension Big Beau produced was complex and unpleasant but also unexpectedly helpful for discovering ourselves in a strange pressure-filled kind of way.

There was another fantastic martial artist among us, yet none of us had a clue about his depth of compassion and wisdom or his martial skill. The first two men to join us walked onto the trail saddle and managed to simply move away from Beau without much of an exchange. And Beau left them alone as soon as they came onto the high ground. The third one to arrive was Harmon, who hiked with a walking staff. Surprisingly, it was not high tech lightweight metal like several others had but solid hard wood. I wondered why anyone would carry something so heavy on a serious hike. The thought had vanished early in the journey until this moment when Harmon stepped onto the saddle. This time Big Beau continued to yell at him, even though Harmon was only about ten feet away.

Harmon's every step had been methodical and rhythmic, like seasoned hikers move when they get into their stride. He continued walking straight toward Beau without changing his pace or starting to move away as the others had quickly done. His face pointed down, appearing to be watching where he stepped. When he reached the level spot where Beau stood, suddenly, without the slightest forewarning, he jumped straight up into the air and spun around, while emitting a horrific shriek that scarily sliced right into my gut. In that same moment the staff he held whirled with lightning speed across Big Beau's face, an inch from his nose. What a shocking sight to behold, this gentle man now in mid-flight six feet in the air with a warrior ferocity that forced Beau to look up at him. Equally amazing was Big Beau. He did not flinch or even blink and remained motionless the entire time, not from fear, but from sheer discipline, never for a moment taking his eyes away from the dazzling spectacle coming at him.

For the next minute at 14,500-foot elevation, Harmon performed the most dazzling staff kata I have ever seen. Immediately, he reversed his jump spin and again the staff whizzed past Big Beau's nose. He retreated two full steps, only to advance in a ferociously howling overhead thrust, stopping the staff in front of Beau's face. Then he whipped the staff sideways and back to the face, then made the same movements again and again, all with lightning speed and awesome force, voicing howls and shrieks that obliged the mountain ghosts to come to witness. The final few thrusts landed an inch from Beau's temples as though the end of the staff was vibrating like a tuning fork. Harmon finished by twisting down into a pretzel position and then unwinding like a taut spring, whipping the staff backhand in front of Beau's kneecaps. He completed the move with his staff tucked under his arm with his other hand extended forward, fingers pointing up and spread as if saying hi. David Carradine would have been envious of his Shaolin-like poise as Harmon quietly walked over to a boulder and sat down, and all this *with a pack still on his back.*

Big Beau remained standing there for a couple of motionless moments, still powerful and solid. Without the slightest adieu to anyone, the next moment he simply strolled toward the trailhead as if nothing had happened and once there he started yelling at the next hikers down in the distance. This time it was friendlier and more encouraging.

That night after dinner around the campfire, I got to know Harmon, who was a documentary film producer, and found out a little about his and Kamala's lives. They said I was the first person they had met on the journey who even knew about Karlfreid Von Durkheim. They loved that I understood his ideas and could talk with them about their practices.

We never mentioned Beau until the end of the evening when Kamala said something disarming. "We have the right cast of characters here for this play. Beau will come for you, you know that, don't you?" she asked as though it was expected I understood.

"Why do you say that?" I asked with a mixture of surprise and apprehension. Her remark caught me completely off-guard since before that moment I had not shared my personal concerns about Beau with anyone. I did not want to face what she meant even though I felt worried that she was correct.

"Because you are someone who challenges him," she replied. "You are the only one besides Beau who can hold don Eduardo's energy, except Beau practices black magic and you don't. He thinks he can defeat you with his dark energy."

This was the first moment on the journey that I was confronted with how others saw me. I honestly did not realize that Harmon and Kamala saw me in the light they just spoke of, and I instantly recognized my self-centered focus was dampening my broader awareness. Of course others noticed me exactly the same way I did them. We were all beginning to size up each other as a sober consequence of days of travel. Before I could think more about this, however, I had to turn my full attention to the second part of her remarks, what she believed Beau was up to.

"What do you mean?" I was more than a little agitated. "Do you really know that for a fact?" I asked, wanting to understand where they were coming from.

I tended to automatically dismiss anyone who brought up the subject of magic, black or any other kind. With few exceptions I found that the person speaking did not know what they were talking about and/or it was nothing I wanted to listen to. One thing I had clearly learned by that point was that any inauthentic conversation, whether colorful embellishments or tall tales indulged to pass for reality, was absolutely inimical to the shaman's path. Due to the very nature of the art and craft, at least among the shamans I studied with, it was inevitable and natural to often deal directly with the numinous and many aspects of non-ordinary reality. The only way to maintain a healthy sanity and produce growth was to tell the truth about your experience without denial or embellishment, lest you hopelessly confuse yourself. It's not that magic does not exist, or that people do not practice or experience it, rather very, very few have any command of that arena and among those who do even fewer talk about it. What's generally said most of the time is nonsense, so why give it the time of day? On the other hand, coming from these two, I very much wanted to hear what they had to say, regardless.

"Why, Randy, you surprise me," Kamala said. "Do you think he has all that strength from his wilderness school? We thought you recognized that a dark force is running him."

They went on to tell me that they had had dinner with Beau their first night in Lima at the Hotel Bolivar where we collected in those days. That hotel has its own stories. Once terrorists tried to nab me in Lima and the hotel clerks warned me just in time. Many of us had had lots of weird encounters at Hotel Bolivar in Lima over the years, so I had no doubt about the truth of their story. Beau had been to Peru several times before to work with don Eduardo as had most everyone else on this journey. Don Eduardo had introduced Beau to some local sorcerers when he *saw* that Beau was energetically linked with people of similar persuasion. If anyone besides these two people had told me this, I'm not sure what my reaction might have been, but in the light of their story a lot of things suddenly made sense.

I had seen that side in don Eduardo twice before, when perfectly awful people from my perspective had found their way to one of his mesa ceremonies. While I would have been inclined to ignore or marginalize them, don Eduardo would either try to bend their interest toward something positive, or if he *saw* it was useless, direct them to someone he knew, presumably to learn more of the dark arts that interested them. I respected his lack of judgment about it and knew for a fact that he felt no affinity with dark practitioners, in fact he abhorred people he called sorcerers, and he also knew they wished him harm.

Since the term "sorcerer" meant something entirely different and positive to me when I brought it up, he begrudgingly agreed to a distinction between what he meant and what Carlos Castaneda and I meant by sorcerer: a man or woman possessing esoteric knowledge and skills to influence perception and manipulate energy. In this definition the only distinction between shaman and sorcerer is that sorcerers lack the affinity for serving the health of the community by making themselves publicly available for that purpose. Shamans always do that and sorcerers never do. About that we agreed but I insisted that did not mean all sorcerers were dark and in fact quite the opposite. Sometimes this kind of conversation could get a little tense since don Eduardo did not like a lot about Castaneda's writing, but the exact people he meant by "sorcerers" were all too real. In fact, only a year later I would find myself a participant in a battle with those very sorcerers while attempting to defend don Eduardo's life from their hateful attacks. That's another story entirely.

One late night while we were conducting a ceremony out in the desert at one of the famous Nazca floor etchings, I became very agitated from a face-to-face encounter with an utterly real and non-physical Indian who appeared right before my eyes. He was entirely ethereal, opaque and intangible, while also being so fully visual in three-dimensional detail that I could not tell he was incorporeal until he was on top of me. It was weirder than weird. I could easily see the color and patterns on his poncho and the vacant dullness in the eyes that expressed some kind of odd consciousness that was decidedly not alive. And yet "he" was looking directly at me, and had a companion with him. I did not want to be looking at these beings that simply walked out of the desert darkness and approached us, yet I did not dare to look away. It may have been an hallucination, but it was shared and don Eduardo *saw* exactly what I was looking at.

My reaction was aversion yet there was a strange, compelling attraction that I cannot easily explain. These were wondrous times in my life and I was aware of the utterly fantastic, mind-bending and life-altering experiences I was acquiring around don Eduardo and several other Peruvian shamans. I gratefully embraced these years as a whole and disciplined myself not to pick at the parts for a long while. There were many particulars within the world of the shamans I personally found impossible to accept, let alone embrace. There were many experiences in themselves that were

27

unpleasant to terrifying that I would never want to repeat. These kinds of experiences were far outweighed, however, by light-filled, enlightening and heart-affirming encounters, which in the whole provided me a wide-ranging education. That night in the desert, however, I had no idea what I had done at don Eduardo's mesa to invite these entities since I had not intentionally called anyone or anything to me. Yet there they were, standing in front of us. Don Eduardo said they were responding to our mesa light in the darkness, the exact reason we were there and we had attracted their interest. Our ceremony in this remote ancient desert site had called them to us. Now *it was up to me to answer them.*

"Move them along, Compadre, now, before they challenge our mesa. We don't want the fight," don Eduardo growled loudly.

Although I understood don Eduardo, I had no idea what I was supposed to do. What I remember is that unbidden thoughts just arrived in my head. In my mind I saw that these two beings came from an area farther up north toward Paracas Bay. The light of our mesa ceremony had attracted them, but essentially they were heading toward and beyond us anyway. That was it. I simply recognized these beings were still on their way home, traveling north. Somehow having these thoughts of recognition was enough. I watched them move directly toward me. I still don't know if it was right or wrong, but I did not move since I was in my stance of power next to the mesa and felt there was no place safer. As I watched him move toward me from thirty feet away, I almost had a heart attack. He moved steadily toward me until finally I braced myself for being bumped into. Complete with poncho, no hat, scraggly hair and vacant eyes looking straight ahead, he *passed through my shoulder*. His companion moved in tandem ten feet to the other side of don Eduardo and they both disappeared into the dark desert chaparral behind us.

"They accepted your blessing," don Eduardo said, and continued his mesa rituals. "You moved them along and they accepted."

We got through that night OK but the next morning I was still chewing on it when Don Eduardo came over and sat by me, knowing exactly what was on my mind. Don Eduardo carefully explained to me that the universe is comprised of light and dark forces and any attempt to eliminate either could only bring disharmony and possibly disaster to the shaman.

"You did right, last night," he proclaimed. "In truth they are only dark forces when they oppose you. Otherwise they are simply there. You did not arouse their hostility while calmly facing them directly. They saw you had no fight with them therefore they had none with you."

He said shamans believe they must acknowledge the dark forces' rightful place in our universe and in fact their existence allows for the opposite, the world of light. This is a universal idea not unique to don Eduardo's shamanism, but the personal emphasis he gave is exceptional if not strange.

"They would resent you for denying their reality," he said, "That kind of shaman wouldn't last long. You saluted them on their way home; otherwise they would have turned on us for denying them. Since they have chosen to dwell for however long in the desert, it is their house we visit when we go there. Treat them with respectful indifference and they will usually leave you alone."

Don Eduardo told me I had been respectful to their presence without fearing them or trying to draw them to us, either intentionally or by making a mistake. That's essentially how it's done, he said. The shaman labors for an entire life to uphold the strength of the light but also "sadly" realizes that to do so only adds to the dark at the universal level.

"They could have caused us trouble, but we gave them nothing to fight. How could it be any other way?" he rhetorically asked me. "Only the dark allows us to recognize the light. Only both give us the universe we inhabit. Those desert ghouls could have wanted us for dinner, but instead granted us the same existence we granted them. It was more than enough for both of us. Had you denied them it would have been different."

His comments reflect the inherent relationship between the light and dark dimensions of reality that universal spiritual systems (and contemporary astrophysics) report, except the shaman emphasized the inevitable and therefore natural co-existence of both. According to the shaman, we have no choice about the fact that both exist, only the choice about which side we uphold and the manner in which we do it. Ultimately the shaman recognizes that *it makes no difference in the universal picture* which side one upholds. Then what difference does it make, I asked, if either choice reveals and even manifests its opposite?

"The only difference is a personal one," Eduardo replied. "I am happy and strong as a shaman. Why would I want anything else?"

To me this was no mere philosophical point. His explanation provided me an intellectual bridge between my behavior with the shamans to my then life in Northern California as a therapist. Therapy sessions do not engage the same activities as performing ancient ceremonies in the desert and yet both can be exercises with similar purposes. Get to the high ground, at least higher than where the conflict is taking place. In both worlds I had no illusions that sometimes things would go well, and other times disappointingly wrong. All that mattered was doing my best against clear criteria and being honest about the results.

"Someday much stronger entities will come for you," he said, "and you must learn to handle them. It's always been that way. The shaman lights his filaments with San Pedro and his life's work. Eventually his brightness draws the attention of the old sorcerers, people like you and me who escaped death but did not make it to heaven." (Yes, he actually used that word with little resemblance to its Christian meaning.) "They will come to feed on your light when your energy body becomes so bright that they cannot resist. For them you are a meal placed before their table and you will be a morsel they swallow if you cannot stand your ground. For that you will need *power*."

This explanation was the basis that led to an eventual journey to Marcawasi and likely why he insisted that his initiation must take place there. Don Eduardo had said that it was the position of his lineage not to wait for the old sorcerers to come to you, but to go to Marcawasi and face them directly. If you succeeded, much *power* would flow to you and if you failed you were never much of a shaman anyway. The shaman did not give me a choice about this direction, no more than his teachers had given him, but he did not force it upon me. It was my choice whether to pursue his teaching but not mine to adjust the curriculum, at least at that point in time.

Whatever was the actual story, there was no question that Big Beau was frequently larger than life and propelled by an energy that possessed him, whatever the source, and that very kind of being-ness is often exactly how one behaves when driven by forces other than your own singular volition. I remarked to Kamala and Harmon that I would just as soon ignore Beau and stay out of his path and simply tend to my own process.

"That's very foolish, Randy," Kamala said dryly. "You're not sure of your own power and that makes you irresistible to him. This is the journey where you are destined to find your power, or lose it. He sees that and he will try to take yours if he can."

Oh great! Now what? The clearest seer on our journey had just told me a nightmare that I could not ignore, one I did not want to deal with. I would have to face a nemesis with the potential for facing dark magic at the hands of someone who knows how to use it. What happened to simple initiations where some guru waves a peacock feather across your face and everything is supposed to be hunky dory thereafter? *Hold on, partner*, I surely said to myself.

Aren't you the guy who distrusts that kind of fluff stuff and never saw it doing much for anyone anyway? I continued to myself. Aren't you the guy who needed proof at the hands of real shamans that something real had occurred before you would accept being initiated? Well, here you are, brother, so don't flake now!

31

I may or may not have had those exact thoughts but I remember those exact feelings and decided then and there that "yes" was my answer. I did indeed require something beyond the ordinary to happen, exactly like this journey, for me to accept being initiated, even though I am certain I was not at all clear what exactly that meant.

The Spirit had directed me in a vision and subsequent synchronisms to be exactly where I was. *I knew this to be true in my bones, without a doubt.* This woman and her gentle husband read me correctly. This journey was for me to learn something about myself, and Beau was sent by The Spirit to make certain that I did. If I could not deal with him, respecting and empowering him without fearing him or bowing to his outrageous dominance, then I would be no shaman. The die was cast and my work was before me. We enacted this ritualistic journey walking the Inca trail to have something happen. I believe that everyone on that journey felt the same if only from his or her own perspective. I would face Beau when the moment was right; I knew there was no guarantee it would turn out well, and yet I must trust that it would. Looking into Kamala and Harmon's eyes I could tell everything was being arranged. There was no other way I could have arrived at such a tender and delicious moment with these two beautiful beings. My trust rekindled in those moments. Well, mostly.

But what if I fail? Why, real breakdown could happen . . .and this isn't fair . . .

Still my mind would not quite leave me alone even though I knew that everything was perfect. No guarantee, a lot at risk, a lot worth cherishing without exactly knowing how to do that. Yes, this was truly an initiation journey that only The Spirit could have orchestrated, although Shaman Alberto Villoldo along with don Eduardo originally called everyone together. As far as I was concerned we were forever in their debt.

As if listening to my thoughts, Kamala and Harmon said I was getting everything I asked for on this journey, referring to my seriousness about investigating and claiming the world of the shaman. I have to say that everyone got that about me whether or not you liked me. No one questioned my utter seriousness about all of this, not to say it placed me beyond criticism nor did everyone automatically accept my views. Perhaps one of my essential differences with Big Beau was I never sought everyone's agreement about my views, only their trust at certain moments.

"If Beau succeeds at humiliating you," they went on to say, "don Eduardo may have no choice except to initiate him, not to mention that you will lose your power to a man, who will abuse you like a cheap whore. The Spirit and *power* will present you the move and we will send you our prayers that you will be strong enough when the moment arrives."

"Cheap whore?" Wow. Kamala did not mince her words and Harmon had already made it clear what I would face. Her phrase made me shudder and I recalled reading T.E. Lawrence when the Arabian sheik became insanely jealous of his growing reputation and sent his men to rape Lawrence, which they did, pitilessly again and again to break his spirit. I understood Kamala all too well. I remember climbing into my sleeping bag feeling energized and threatened at the same time. Harmon and Kamala had completely caught me by surprise, both by their acknowledgement and their warning, and they knew it. There were at least three, maybe four others on this journey equally or more qualified than me to be initiated by don Eduardo. Personally speaking, I did not regard Beau as one of them, although more than a few times he would show me why he thought he was the next Wizard of the Four Winds, and in those moments earn my complete respect though never my allegiance.

I knew, at least believed, I could not match Big Beau in a physical confrontation and any slips on my part to let that happen would be a defeat, no matter the outcome. The luminous warrior could never be about combat. Yet somehow I had to stand him down and in a way that completely stopped him and settled it with finality. The unknown would be when, how? I knew that I had to remain vigilant for the moment that would reveal itself.

Somehow I would have to grab a spontaneous opportunity and make it happen on my own terms. Still I groaned settling into my sleeping bag. A face-to-face showdown with a real nemesis I had not signed up for. Or had I?

I had encountered power with fearful overtones and command of black magic a few times in Peru and I had already turned it down. The very first time I went to Peru to work with don Eduardo, his then superlative apprentice, Alberto, arranged for us all to pay a visit to an up-and-coming jungle shaman apprentice, Augustine Rivas. At that time Augustine was not the world-renowned master he later became. In subsequent years his notoriety grew during the amazing adventures Alberto, Lorena and I arranged with him. But at that time he was still an apprentice to a very old and crusty medicine man I learned later was a formidable sorcerer in the Amazon medicine world. Don Ramon took a strong disliking to me although it was entirely impersonal, friendly even, and that's why it was dangerous. I had not a clue until it happened, and I was still very green about reading the real intentions of very powerful indigenous medicine people. Suffice it to say they don't think like Westerners and they do not see the same world we do, standing together talking. Later I learned he had a lifelong reputation of hammering on the strong younger men when they came around and if they survived he left them alone. During ceremony he decided to "test" me and I believe tried to capture my energy body.

In another series of tales, I will describe the profound and sometimes dark powers of the jungle shamans and my intense experiences during five years of travel. I cannot tell those stories and hope to be understood without first presenting these tales to provide a context. For now I will just say that I survived an attack in a ceremony that removed any question for me about what others call black magic. It can indeed be real. I do not personally like the term "black magic" since it is so widely used in every direction that it retains no precise meaning and has great potential to confuse.

Still I use it because that is exactly the phrase the shamans of Peru used.

In my experience the following is what's meant by black magic. *It's understood* that a singularly focused mind with a lot of emotional and psychic juice, however one acquires it, can direct a kind of psychic energy toward anyone they choose. It's only black when the intentions are black and shamans will point out we all send energy all the time to each other. Magic is only a matter of degree, impact, and purposeful outcome. Love directed thoughts, for example, one of the hallmarks of the Shaman don Eduardo's shamanic system, are similar intentional energy, except they come from our Source and we can only pass it along and thereby extend the creation of light. We do not "create" loving thoughts, rather we share them, receive them, and participate in what comes from beyond us. Hateful, intentionally damaging thoughts and intentions, on the other hand, are thought to be individually selected: the hallmark of black magic with its origins in the dark forces of the universe also expressed through personal intention. Shamans and spiritual practitioners of many kinds well understand this. Intention is just a concept until one learns a method of delivery. The consequences and effects, both for sender and receiver, depend on many things that will shape the reality of the final experience. From that first journey to Peru forward I never had any doubt about the reality of energy practitioners who interact with inter-dimensional fields and bring to bear personal intentions with an impact that is normally beyond the pale of what we accept as real. Shamans and sorcerers direct energy for whatever purpose they choose and in one way or another it comes back to them.

The question for me was: What is left that I can accept from the heritage of the *shaman*? Finally, was it only magic, learning to manipulate the invisible forces for personal power, or was there something more eternal and holy such as what I believed don Eduardo sometimes displayed? Don Eduardo had pledged that he would experientially answer my question with a clarity that could not be denied, something he had solemnly promised he would do at Marcawasi, so that I could authentically choose. He wanted me to be a shaman, I knew that, and he very much wanted me to see, to understand and to be in full possession of what it was truly about: why it had remained alive in continuous practice for arguably twenty-five thousand years. But all this was far from simple. He would keep his promise and indeed place me at choice about *power*, about the heritage of the shaman, and with Big Beau.

Walking the Lagoon

One of the initiations occurred on a foggy and wispy afternoon while we stood around butt-naked on shimmering banks of rolling granite waiting our turn to walk the lagoon. More than a few of the initiations of don Eduardo, as well as other shamans I had worked with in Peru, required one to be naked in front of others. Then and now I had mixed reactions about it. I had no personal objections to nudity, I was not embarrassed about my body and certainly the many initiations involving water were best performed without clothes. Over the years I had come to recognize the profound importance of nakedness and being utterly exposed to the elements at particular moments in the shamanic path. With groups of Westerners, however, ceremonies can quickly devolve to playfulness and erotic behavior and while there's nothing wrong with either, it's a different direction than working toward fulfilling the initiation. In this group that was never a concern. These were superbly self-disciplined people, mentally, emotionally, and spiritually, in spite of our many differences about what that meant. When it came time for ceremony with don Eduardo, no one had any other agenda than fulfilling their part. That's been very rare in my experience.

Crystal clear water seeped from underneath the granite into pockets of ice water along the enormous mountaintop. The initiation required one to solemnly walk an invisible path neck level through the lagoon, about seventy yards in all, without showing any trace of discomfort or imbalance while retaining a presence that don Eduardo would recognize. Essentially you simply had to look good doing it, displaying yourself as someone steadfast with a resolve that overcame the effects of the environment. From the shore don Eduardo would blow his holy water and chant and rattle while we walked the lagoon, circling around a distant rock protruding from the water and then walking back to his staff on the shore. Many slipped in the icy water, a few, as soon as they stepped in. One person had intense convulsions that could threaten hypothermia. A few shivered so intensely on the bank of the lagoon that they had to grab their ponchos or clothes, which signaled utter defeat of their complete initiation.

The two most powerful women in the group completed their walks and left us speechless with their flawless elegance. I thought of the Mists of Avalon as they appeared to silently glide through dark clear water without a ripple. When they stepped onto the shore, Botticelli's Venus emerging from the sea froth was pale in comparison to their stunning presence as they dripped icy water and acted as if they were emerging onto a Hawaiian beach. Don Eduardo beamed his salute to each of them, blowing his fragrant waters up and down their bodies, front and back, which provided a sublime touch to an already exotic scene. My delicious appreciation for these unforgettable moments was all too short-lived when don Eduardo abruptly halted my reverie. Pointing to me with his rattle, he called my name and began chanting. In an instant the entire scene turned into something lucidly intense, engulfing me in a supercharged adrenaline state. I shifted from observer to participant and readied my mind "to strut my hour upon the stage" and perhaps to be heard and seen from no more. There were very few things in life that I dreaded more than cold water!

Don Eduardo called me to stand beside his staff and face the water while he began the ritual. Thankfully, I felt honored to be there and I held that feeling to concentrate my mind and empty it of all thoughts. After a brief staging before don Eduardo at the shore, I stepped into the water and to this day I have a hard time remembering anything except my focusing on that rock and taking my next step. Each breath was so intense and deeply felt that everything disappeared around me except that rock, which appeared like a sentinel jutting through glass. It was as if I were looking through a tunnel; it was all I could see and all I cared about. All I could hear was a steady loud ringing in my ears. How silent and tender that rock appeared; I could almost lick its smooth gray surface while I steadily navigated around it. For an instant I lost all my bearings as I lost my focus on the rock. Then my vision shifted and all I could see was don Eduardo's staff, again as though I were looking through a tunnel, which became my next beacon. Eventually I emerged from the water certain that I had not missed a step nor wandered from my intent, but I was extremely disoriented as I stepped from the water onto solid and dry ground. I had a difficult time standing up and my vision was constricted as though it was still searching for the rock or the staff. I was on the shore but not yet fully accepting that I was there. My body wanted to continue walking in the water, but the earth kept lifting into my feet, making my knees wobble.

It did not feel at all like I was in the same world I had left, and soon my bare feet felt it was mandatory to revere the ground I walked on. The earth felt sacred and I truly felt reverent standing on her. Stepping into the air was like stepping into a warm blanket and the feeling was joyful, although it made me conscious that I was disoriented and still grasping where I was. Perhaps even before entering the water I slipped into a steadfast trance with a fierce determination to allow nothing to enter my mind except taking my next step. Slowly the world around me entered my awareness and came into focus. Gradually I could see, hear and feel don Eduardo joyfully dancing, rattling and chanting around me while spitting cloudbursts of his sacred waters up and down my front and back.

"Look between your legs," don Eduardo said, still sounding farther away than he was.

He blew his fragrances repeatedly across my chest while chanting and rattling as if he were utterly delighted. What a luxurious feeling and aroma penetrated my lungs with a camphor unique to don Eduardo. It was his smell, his exotic elixir and fragrance that left me feeling blessed. Eventually my mind caught up to his words.

What did he say? I asked myself in disbelief. Naw, he couldn't have said that, I must have thought to myself as I gingerly felt the welcome soil beneath my feet that was surprisingly foreign but slowly orienting me to dry land.

"Look down," don Eduardo said and laughed warmly as he whistled and rattled.

I was still slow to comprehend his meaning until I looked straight in front of me at two women, the two who had already emerged from the water, who were staring directly at my genitals with the most serious priestess look imaginable. In addition to being outrageously beautiful and naked, these two very dissimilar women had power and presence that caused everyone to respect them, to fear them, or both, making their stare something that demanded my correct response without my having any idea what it was. Following their eyes I looked down and saw that my penis was erect. I laughed inside as I looked back at the women whose eyes met mine and we all smiled together. The men who had gone before me all joked about their disappearing penis from being in that icy water. I was more than surprised to see my own, erect and visible. It was years later, however, before I understood the initiation.

CHAPTER THREE

Initiation Fire Ceremony at Marcawasi

As the sun was setting behind the towering walls, I was grateful that it had been a warm and beautiful day. We were at the top of the world and it felt like that: glorious, surreal and utterly real, ancient and mysterious at the same time. It was a little like Haleakala Crater and a few other power spots I have visited, where simply sitting on a rock exuded energy. Often there was a feeling followed by something moving in the corner of your eye, except in this place there would actually be something real there. I could hear the near and distant sounds of people moving around camp; this gigantic bowl had a sonic resonance that caused voices and sounds to bounce off the walls, confusing the direction of their origin. Even though we were spread out for a hundred yards we could hear each other's conversations, and it bonded us in a unique way.

Due to the sonic closeness within the bowl I was slow to notice that I was literally out on the edge, alone. On the first morning I soon realized that everyone except me had set up tents near don Eduardo's tent and I was directly across the bowl from them. I thought about that as I reclined comfortably on a smooth rock next to my tent; the rock lifted me seamlessly from the ground at the perfect height for a comfortable chair. My small backpacking tent was the farthest away from don Eduardo's big orange pavilion with its high center pole and tassels atop a knoll, which reminded me of medieval knights preparing for a joust. Packhorses had brought it up. I guessed that he had entrusted someone in the village to provide him a tent and was likely surprised by it as well. None of the surroundings complimented or agreed with its presence. This tent was so out of place that either the commanding environment

41

swallowed it completely and it disappeared, or it dominated the view so that you noticed nothing else.

When I dropped my judgment that somebody's gaudy taste had ambushed don Eduardo, I had to admit it enriched our cognitive dissonance, a vitally critical necessity for the occasion. Normalcy was the enemy here: the predictable, the everyday tried and true. The shaman well knows that ANY routine elicits a dampening energy that countermands our purpose for being at Marcawasi. Getting out of your mind, out of your own way of prejudices and preconceived reality is the necessary path if you seek to experience the ecstasy of the shaman and their navigated realities. Ordinary reality and ordinary expectations make it impossible to achieve escape velocity for loftier altitudes, and it must be exited entirely, though without causing harm to yourself or others. The shaman leaves behind a normal mind to manifest joy, health and well-being. Most consider that a contradiction and therein lies the sacred craft and artistry of the shaman. Cognitive dissonance is mandatory and high on the list of necessary ingredients for contact with the ineffable and Zen masters among others understand this practice as well as shamans, the masters of cosmic drama.

The shamans call such contact the *nagual*: direct contact with and being acted upon by *power, sustained moments when ordinary reality changes with physical, mental, and spiritual consequences*. Normal habits, routines and patterns can only uphold normal. That's not what we came for. The tent very quickly fit right in. Whatever we had to say about it, normal was not part of the equation.

What an exquisite environment to find myself in! I was grateful, both for this amazing time and for how I felt. I felt blessed. It was more humbling than arrogant, and the strong peaceful feeling only heightened my gratitude. As the sun went down and gigantic shadows climbed the enormous walls around me, I knew I was ready to face the fire ceremony. During my meditation I had taken an inventory of my behavior that had brought me to this place.

Though not perfect, I had done what I could in a manner worthy of the quest. I recognized that Kamala and Harmon's assessment of me was essentially correct. I was not yet confident about my power. Not only that, a lot of the time I was not even certain what it meant. My power? What power? I thought *power* was something that only belonged to The Spirit. How could anyone but a fool take personal credit? Looking at personal power honestly had produced a freedom.

The shaman's idea about *power* was elusive for me. Yet I had seen *power* move through don Eduardo enough times to recognize there was something natural about my dilemma, and I trusted that it would clarify itself sooner or later. The only way I had been able to define *power* was to accept the shaman's explanation: *Power is when the shaman "beckons" Spirit(s) to act through him/her. Power is when something happens that does not fit within what is ordinarily considered possible, and most especially when the shaman intends it.* These moments are also known as the *nagual*, the *alternate* reality very similar to our ordinary world in appearance though fundamentally different. All the rules are reversed. The spiritual, the energy and the abstract are the senior absolutes that define the *nagual* reality and not the physical/material, such as in our normal world. In the *nagual* impossible things naturally happen and these so-called impossibilities are integral within an expanded reality of which we are a part, though we seldom realize it. The *nagual* is the abstract and impersonal manifestation of The Spirit that comes forward and either whacks or blesses the shaman with high frequency energy and communication.

Even though these ideas made clear intellectual sense, it had not brought me any peace or practical understanding.

"You witnessed *power* last night at your own hands," don Eduardo once remarked to me, "yet still you ask me what it is."

"But don Eduardo," I said with genuine concern, "if it was at my hands, then how come I have a hard time believing last night actually happened, let alone that I could remotely know how to make it happen again?"

"That's your problem," he said a little curtly. "You don't believe in your own experience. It's not important you know how to make it happen again. It's important you recognize what occurred. *Power* is a force that acts on us. It's what we pray for, to be acted upon by *power* to make our intentions happen. Very few shamans know *exactly* how *power* will present itself. How could they? If they did, they would be one and the same as *power*. Only the Divine Master (the Resurrected Jesus) is that! (Don Eduardo believed that more than a few shamans had escaped personal death, but Jesus was the only one to accomplish it perfectly within God's love by resuscitating himself from corporeal death, something only God's love could accomplish and not the same move as the shaman or the sorcerer, who escape physical death in the first place.) The shaman *intends* what *power* has guided him to intend. That's what you did last night at the mesa. *Power* answered your intentions that were given you by *power*."

We were talking about the previous night's ceremony when don Eduardo served me nine seashells of a black viscous tobacco juice mixed with cane alcohol, perfumes and other stimulants. I stood before the shaman at his mesa, invariably because I had been called before him during a San Pedro ceremony. I inserted (carefully!) the long thin leg of the shell into my nostril and leaned my head back. The secret trick was to never try to snort it and not to let myself cough. I had to simply let it roll all the way down the back of my throat. To most who try it, this experience is not only disgusting but also physically revolting and even worse than it sounds. It often produces an intense gagging with various physical reactions that few want to repeat. The shaman will serve the nose juice during ceremony for various purposes including healing, helping to incite vision with the spiritual eye, cleansing on many levels and also "testing." On rare occasions it can be used to teach a lesson, such as the time a man kept jumping up during ceremony, a shallow charade of acting out the jaguar and pawing at the women nearby. Don Eduardo called him over and asked him to face the direction of the jaguar, *away from the mesa,* and then served him a shell of the nose juice to honor the great jaguar shaman in our midst. He immediately vomited several times and learned something about humility. At least he soon became congruent with the flow of the ceremony.

The shaman claims that anyone, if they focus properly, can "easily handle" one, sometimes two shells of the nose juice and receive benefit, especially the heightening visions during San Pedro ceremonies. Rarely will the shaman give even the hardiest participant more than three or four shells. Five to seven are considered serious tests that will cause most anyone to violently vomit eventually. The point is to hold it long enough to respectfully stand before the shaman with strength and dignity for however long the mood and energy require. Nine is rare and reserved for special occasions of an initiatory nature. It's been done that way for hundreds of years. If someone wants to be a shaman, and a shaman accepts his/her request, there are a lot of rituals, initiations and tests that will determine that person's qualifications for the job.

My general attitude was that any authentic protocol used continuously for centuries must be there because it works. I have evolved that attitude over the years and at the time that's how I approached the world of the Peruvian shamans. I took things exactly as the shamans presented them. To do otherwise was to judge and there's no way a shaman would allow me into their world with such an attitude. I never abandoned my discernment, however, and if anything, don Eduardo respected that in me. I always looked for deeper meanings and often found them, though not always to my liking. The nose juice did indeed cause visions. With a little concentration or sheer determination, I could ignore any taste or feeling it caused, control my stomach, and then try to enjoy what would rather quickly overwhelm me. The first requirement was simply to remain on my feet and if I did not get nauseous or dizzy then the enhancement for *seeing* energy was more than worth it.

Don Eduardo was deeply moved to see me still on my feet after nine nose juices, although that hardly captures what it was truly like in those moments of "standing" in front of this shaman's mesa at the height of a ceremony. Soaring powerfully like an intoxicated eagle into a magnificent thunderstorm and leaping from nine hundred feet above the canyon floor into a thunderhead with lightning bolts flying in my face is metaphorically more apt an explanation. If I had a body in this world I had no clue of any such thing. While expanding into this non- localized self-identity, I never abandoned my *intention* to "stand before the shaman" nor did I allow my mind to lose connection with that purpose and that's the point to this practice as far as I understand it. What moves the shaman is when he *sees* the initiate's connection to him and his mesa overrides the physical demands of the occasion. I have seen it time and time again. If your heart is sincere at whatever level of understanding you possess and you do not judge it, then the nose juice at least for one or two shells, sometimes more, will be kind to you. You may say later that it wasn't so bad and you found some value in the experience. On the other hand, if you approach it with disgust, well, that's pretty much what you get, although people would often report they still received something of value.

I was already in a heightened state and the nose juice took me to another dimension entirely. My vision exploded with keen and brilliant perception both in a normal and extraordinary sense. I was able to not only see exceptionally well in the dark, but also what was "in the dark" that normally remained outside my perception. Don Eduardo motioned for me to sit next to him behind the mesa. How I navigated to sit next to him must have been more magical than I could appreciate at the time.

Looking at the circle from behind his mesa, and more precisely at the people who comprised "the circle," became a unified energy field that connected and surrounded everyone within a lattice of colorful gossamer webs. This astonishing view presented me with another aspect of the shaman's reality and the energetic universe in which he dwells. Factually speaking, don Eduardo's "mesa" was simply a blanket on the ground with a hundred or so objects set in a particular order of meaningful relationships and precise geometric patterns. Usually ten or more swords, knives and staffs were stabbed into the ground in front of the mesa and in back of him as well. Shamanically speaking, the objects each hold a particular energy and particular intent or meaning and were used by the shaman as tools, and no longer existed as symbols. Don Eduardo referred to his mesa as his "control panel" and he meant this quite literally when he worked with *power* during San Pedro ceremonies.

San Pedro refers to the mescaline psychoactive cactus native to Peru and the high desert of the Andes. The shamans of Peru believe that the spiritual entity *mescalito* is the *power* in residence within the cactus and definitely a HE, who will interact with the shaman if he eats or drinks the cactus in a *properly prepared, ritual manner.* Just about anyone can experience the psychoactive effects of the cactus and never know anything about encountering *mescalito*. Such inter-dimensional contact is rarefied territory reserved for shamans who have been cultivating this relationship for countless generations and passing it on to their apprentices. This is no idle myth, rather something so serious and consequential that it is best entered with reverence and respect, knowing full well you seek audience with a benefactor well beyond your ability to understand and whose effects you will never get over. In other words, a non-indigenous sentient life form that *possesses knowledge and power* and exists in an alternate dimension of reality with the potential to transfer that power to a shaman in our world, someone who is purified enough to receive it.

The only way an aspiring shaman knows if he or she meets the criteria to encounter *mescalito* or receive *power*, is to finally make direct contact and find out what happens. This is rarely talked about but the initial encounter with *mescalito* is almost always dangerous because nothing prepares you fully for the experience. It is simply beyond anything you had ever conceived possible and consequently the experience is almost always disturbing. The only question is: Will the disturbance be profoundly helpful or just plain disturbing? It's been reported that way in shaman traditions and it is my testament as well. Nothing prepares you completely and your nerves, your mental, emotional and physical capacities will tell you whether you ever wish for an encore of being acted directly upon in an utterly impossible manner that cannot be denied. If the apprentice is fortunate, it will occur when his benefactor is delivering hands-on training and is present to ensure that the apprentice's mind isn't shattered and to calm the apprentice's nerves before they reach detrimental proportions of fear. No one meets *mescalito* and says they were fully prepared for it but in the same breath all say they are grateful to have prepared whatever they did. Shamans uphold only what they can corroborate within their own experience, and there are records of their ceremonial relationship with the San Pedro cactus that go back thousands of years. Fossil records indicate the San Pedro cactus did not exist on the earth before 50,000 years ago and then it suddenly appeared. Shamans say the spores of the cactus arrived from the stars.

"Now you must help those sitting before you," the Shaman said imperatively, as though I already knew what he was talking about. "What do you *see* on the mesa?" don Eduardo asked.

I could not answer him in any rational mode of thinking since my normal cognitive functions had long since vacated and I was not even sure he had asked me in words. I was in two worlds at once and they sometimes blurred together, requiring great concentration to know what I was doing or thinking or where I was. Something in me looked down on the mesa and pointed with a gesture at the object that had an enchanting and luminous vaporous aura around it as if a light bulb were lit underneath it. My enchantment in seeing the object was immediately interrupted with a command almost shouted at me with a sense of urgency.

"Then send it!" he demanded as though I knew what he meant. "*See* the person with the rabbit's light on them. *See* them and command it and it will go."

The object I had pointed to was a rabbit's foot, one of the dozens of power objects on the mesa, and I had no conscious thought other than focusing on the light around it. I'm sure I did not even recognize the particular object until Eduardo's command told me what it was. Something in me looked up to *see* the same exact hue of soft whitish vapor around the little furry object on the mesa cloth was also around the shoulders of a man in the circle. Since the entire backdrop all around us was pure dark wilderness, this misty light easily stood out. When I looked down again at the mesa I *saw* the rabbit foot "get up and walk," no, it actually "ran" across the circle and appeared to jump onto the shoulders of this same man. I simply witnessed it as though I was watching something natural. It traveled across the circle and disappeared into this man, who soon thereafter stood up and approached the mesa. He appropriately walked in a clockwise direction, and came and knelt before us. Speaking from a place much deeper than ordinary conversation, he then thanked don Eduardo for taking an enormous load off his shoulders. There had been no conversation with him about anything, and I do not believe he was consciously aware a power object had visited him from don Eduardo's mesa, except he felt it.

This same scenario repeated itself many times and I stayed with it. Each time a different mesa power object would light up and when I recognized it, don Eduardo would voice something like: "ahhh" and mutter words like "compadre" and alternately chant familiar and incomprehensible incantations particular to that object. Another moment and his powerful arm would swoop down over the mesa and grab one of his flasks filled with magical ingredients for very specific purposes. His other arm would swing around and grab the cork before the flask arrived to his lips. He would then throw his head back and gulp enormous swigs, only to then explode with a melodious roar, turning the contents into a vaporous mist onto the mesa and onto the people in the circle. The smells and scents always affected us in many ways. Then he would grab his ceremonial pipe and repeat the entire performance, directing the "smoke" of *the entity Tobacco* into his objects on the mesa and to affect those sitting in his circle. I'm not talking about our Western smoking habits here, but rather something energetic and very real. Sitting anywhere in the circle, even thirty feet away, when the shaman directed his pipe smoke at us something tangible landed on us. The jungle shamans are the most notorious for using the breath and tobacco smoke to attack their enemies, but I only saw don Eduardo do it to affect people with positive spiritual energy. He was very precise about that point if only out of concern for his own safety since he believed "the little smoke" that he sent to anyone always came back to him. Another jungle shaman taught me how to use tobacco smoke to attack enemies in the same manner of his ancestors' tribal practices, and no doubt don Eduardo understood this side of things as well.

Again I looked down and saw a mesa object with a light mist shining around it. I looked up at the circle and saw this exact same light, a sort of mist such as fog in headlights, this time in the lap of someone sitting in the circle. Again I looked down at the power object with the same light and again it appeared to turn into something that released animate and live energy in a very specific way. It would stand up and run across the circle and jump onto its own awaiting light that invariably was on a person sitting somewhere in the circle. It became something so familiar and compelling to watch that for some unknown reason my mind did not reject it. "Of course" was my attitude watching a power object that lit up when I placed my attention on it.

The inherent intention of the lighted object was to offer assistance to the targeted person. At least that's what don Eduardo told me was happening. I could only see these light packets travel to someone and trust the meaning was selecting itself since I did not understand the objects with don Eduardo's clarity. Among the many objects precisely placed on Eduardo's mesa were two Christian saints and the resurrected Jesus, as well as rabbit, deer, fox, condor and other animal totems for specific issues. One of the Christian saints might be sent in behalf of someone in the circle to assist a loved one in need, and a rabbit's foot would be sent to locate a lost item and then to tell the shaman where it was to be found. On the other hand, Eduardo might invoke for a particular need an incomprehensible Old World Indian divinity no less real than Jesus. When it landed people would either move, or swoon, or sit up. Each time I could "see" how the power object traveled as a packet of energy. Sometimes I spontaneously understood how a person was affected, as though the information intuitively arrived in my thoughts, complete with considerable detail. I could simply feel that person's emotions with such clarity that information was also conveyed. Some came to the mesa to report and some because they were simply moved to do so, and had nothing to say; don Eduardo would blow his sacred water and oils over them.

I had been deeply moved by what had occurred to be sure. At no time, however, did I have a sense of causing anything to happen. I felt I had been a privileged witness to don Eduardo's shamanism, but he insisted that *power* had moved *through my intentions* that night and I must accept it.

"Don't confuse the shaman's humility with ignorance," don Eduardo said, challenging my disbelief. "That's why they are *power* objects," he added dryly. "What's the use if they don't go when sent? Last night *power* sent them through you."

As I sat on my rock remembering that time in the desert at Nazca when I learned about don Eduardo's mesa objects and *power*, I realized that in a few hours something would happen that would deeply affect me. Looking around at the enormous walls and appreciating the high rolling country around and above us, I mentally thanked the Great Spirit, the Holy Spirit, for everyone's presence on this journey and felt honored to be among such real players, who went well beyond just talking about it.

In the midst of my reflection, Big Beau walked up to me, catching me by surprise drifting in my reflections. I shifted from internal to external attention and came into the moment. He had never come out by my tent before. He said he had ordered a last minute policing of trash so don Eduardo would not have to see anything left by previous visitors. The bowl was littered with trash lying around when we first arrived, most of Peru is the same, and the first thing I had done was clean fifty yards of space around my tent until it was spotless. The higher ground around the bowl was completely *au naturel,* however, with very few signs of intrusion. I looked at Beau with genuine warmth and told him I thought it was an excellent idea and got up to find more trash. His mentioning don Eduardo, however, led me to thinking about another dimension to our journey that was bothering me.

The final ascent to Marcawasi was a full day's hike up a strong incline. The night before our hike we had slept in a barn in the little mountain village and enjoyed our last real meal for a few days, though we did not know it at the time. I have already noted that don Eduardo was sixty years old at the time. He had been born and raised and had lived primarily on the seacoast areas of northwest Peru. In a single day we had taken a bus from the coast to twelve thousand feet and we were now hiking to a seventeen-thousand-foot elevation. Don Eduardo was the one person who rode a horse; everyone else walked with the villagers, who were pulling the packhorses with ropes. About a dozen villagers walked halfway up the mountain with us and then stopped. I did not notice their absence until that evening. The few who came to the top with us told us the mayor had threatened with financial retaliation anyone who worked as a porter for us, even though they had already been commissioned and we were counting on them. In their way of reasoning, walking halfway up the trail satisfied some sense of duty and then abandoning us got the mayor off their back.

Seeing don Eduardo on a horse was novel, since none of us had ever known him to be anything except a strong walker. It seemed he was not enjoying the ride much and did not interact with the hikers. I decided it was discomfort since don Eduardo was a large framed man and appeared much too heavy for this pony size horse bred exclusively for working high altitudes and was surefooted as he gingerly stepped up the trail. I would have preferred to walk any day than sit on a horse. It looked totally uncomfortable to me. The trail required constant stepping up and over the next rock or ledge in a frequently changing terrain.

Somehow I had become oblivious to the trail and buried too deeply in my thoughts. Suddenly and unexpectedly I took a horrible slip and fell. In an instant I was upside down and in midair with that realization freeze-framed in my mind, as I went outside of time and was doused with a horrendous cold-water splash that curdled through my psyche.

Wake up, wake up was the urgent feeling, perhaps even voices that brought my full attention to explode into the now.

In one instant I was in the air and in the next a sharp blow struck the center of my lower back. I had stepped up and onto a rock ledge that was wet. My feet went flying forward with such force they flew higher than my head. I landed on a pointed rocky outcrop, which speared me with a bull's eye onto the high impact plastic water bottle firmly secured in my hip pack. This was the exact reason I carried it there and the second time it saved me from certain injury. I literally bounced up landing on my feet and hardly missed my stride. I heard a few whistles and catcalls from a joking chorus of hikers behind me and I could barely believe what happened only a moment ago. While it was an ancient walking path to the mountaintop I doubt anyone had tended to it in a long while. That was how I was trying to think about it because I anticipated don Eduardo's comment later that evening that an unseen entity had tapped me in a moment when I was vulnerable.

"You must protect yourself better," don Eduardo told me, implying that I had been absent-minded when I should have been paying attention.

I started to get really annoyed, and then took some deep breaths to breathe it away. This kind of correction happened a lot around the shamans and I often had mixed feelings about it. Why couldn't it simply be a slip and fall and nothing to do with supernatural forces? I should be more careful hiking, or not daydream on the trail, or get new hiking boots, anything except some supernatural force singling "me" out to pick on. I did not believe I was that important to warrant such attention from the supernatural, but more likely I was afraid it might be true and disliked that possibility even more.

"It's not supernatural, Amigo," don Eduardo said as though speaking a refrain with an air of conviction and finality. "I have told you before there are only *natural forces* in any universe or they could not be *forces*. The entity that tapped you is real enough, alright, and you can go ask it if you don't believe me."

Don Eduardo's logic often did that, used its own assertion to prove itself. What could I say? I understood phenomenology and so did the shaman though never as an academic topic. Elucidating concepts and weaving stories to orchestrate an actual reality in which to dwell is simply what the shaman does.

On the other hand I knew without a doubt that an accident was never solely accidental having personally investigated this concept with considerable rigor in the lives of several thousand people. A personal inventory with careful investigation of my own life had revealed the precise moment that I ignored or moved against myself in some way prior to anything *accidentally* occurring to me. No matter how convincing the story or the appearance, and my life certainly had many dramas, I always found that I had brought myself to any given moment, no matter how I got there or the story of it. This personal discipline from years of study as a therapist and spiritual trainer gave me a place to stand in a universe that frequently did not make sense. Bottom line, I not only rejected the very idea of victim, I found it too disturbing to accept, not to say that terrible things do not happen that are dearly wished otherwise. As long as I understood there was something inside of me to correct, and that doing so would improve my lot, such as my well being, success and overall happiness in life, then continued navigation made genuine sense to me. At a core level of truth it was my responsibility for the conditions of reality I found myself in and only my own choices governed that.

If, on the other hand, there really are ultimately dark and overpowering forces that will obliterate me no matter what, then an absolute loving Source cannot be possible at the same time.

Both cannot be true and every day is an opportunity to choose which is. I knew that don Eduardo meant to empower me but the idea of this and that entity causing this and that problem was a challenge for me to respect his reality without discarding my own ground of being.

When we got to the top of the mountain, I noticed don Eduardo was aloof because he stayed in his tent most of the time. Now, many years later, I have to wonder if he did not simply need to rest from the high altitude. For some reason none of us had the wit to grant him something so simple, and at the time there was a lot of discussion and rumor about it. It also produced a lot of amazing exchanges among us. Many in the group were remarkable leaders with a great deal to share, and did so when don Eduardo was not filling the space.

Big Beau was not the only grand or even grandiose performer in this crowd, far from it, and we came to know each other fairly well if only because Beau put forward at the beginning of the journey an attitudinal stance that we all shared. We each wanted to know whether we were in the company of real players, and beyond courtesy (well, mostly) no one granted respect to anyone else until it was self-evident they either deserved it, or demanded it in a way that could not be refused. It was up to each of us to make ourselves known. In this sense we all shared some responsibility for Big Beau's outrageous behavior because there was an aspect to it that we all condoned; it was seldom his execution and less seldom his mood, but very often his intent. Who is this other person who declares their readiness for don Eduardo's initiation, and could I trust my back to them? As far as I could tell, with a couple of exceptions, we all came to agree that everyone there had a rightful place. We were very different kinds of folks in most respects, most of us strongly independent, and many accustomed to being in charge. The depth and range of delicious self-portraits everyone presented would make Chaucer's pilgrims from his *Canterbury Tales* appear boring.

Even though a few of us recognized a hardball wisdom in don Eduardo's refusal for much interaction with us except when we were doing group work, it was harder to understand why he avoided us for the simple things, such as sharing tea in the evening. His withdrawal from participation, even on a tribal basis, caused considerable turmoil with everyone; no one, including me, understood it. None of us had ever seen that kind of behavior from him before, and without realizing it, we had always taken for granted that this profound, charismatic and powerful man would be moving among us, setting the mood, the tone, the level of conversation and orchestrating the play. After all, he was the shaman and utterly delightful and warmly engaging in normal life and bigger than life during ceremonies and training. Everything was supposed to move around him, wasn't it? Not this time. Don Eduardo was available and magnificent during each initiation he set before us, and then he was gone, sometimes even taking his meals (until we ran out of food!) in his tent. His absence left a huge vacuum and as a result we had a lot of time to spend with each other and within our own inner worlds.

Twilight finally gave way to darkness as I drifted in my thoughts, still reclining on my rock next to my tent. The last rays of the sun had disappeared entirely and I was now looking up at complete pitch-black sky and no moon whatsoever. The brilliance of the stars overhead was intensely luminous, enveloping the granite walls with shimmering starlight from a cloudless night. Many people were standing in front of their tents waiting for don Eduardo to call everyone to circle for the initiation fire ceremony. We had gathered an enormous pile of wood for the ceremonial fire, which was no small feat at this altitude. There was hardly any wood nearby and we foraged a great distance to bring it in. Only after we arrived at Marcawasi did we realize the shortage of porters. A dozen villagers had simply dropped back off the trail and gone unnoticed, leaving three teenagers and a young woman from the village to manage our kitchen: a board set between two rocks in front of a small dilapidated tent that contained our meager provisions. They had brought all they could carry, each pulling a packhorse they had hastily loaded with mostly fruit and cereal at the last minute, but they had no wood, which the porters usually provided.

Somehow a major breakdown had occurred in the village pub the previous night, and don Eduardo had pissed off the village mayor about what we were doing there, or so the gossip went around the camp. As the story went, several men from our group were in the adobe cinderblock pub, the sole bar in this remote village, which was equipped with an ice chest and several tables. It was owned by the village mayor and also served as his place for official business. While having a last beer with don Eduardo, they watched him get into an argument with the mayor, so the rumor had some substance to it. The mayor had suddenly approached and demanded that don Eduardo pay a tax of some sort and it led to a loud exchange. When one shaman travels to another area, it is the ancient custom that the visiting shaman announces him/herself *to the local shaman* and asks permission to do ceremonial work in his or her area. Traditionally, an honorary payment would be made to the local shaman to acknowledge permission has been sought and granted. In fact and practice, however, it had not been that simple in most of Peru since the time of the Incas. The problem was that in modern times it was seldom clear which shaman influenced which dominion or area. Some might be famous among the people beyond their hometown, and most shamans moved around for work and travel and so forth. Was their hometown their only shamanic province, and did they have to ask permission every time they traveled, and if so of whom?

I knew don Eduardo to be a practical man (he was a fisherman and a non-academic archaeologist), and also knew he probably would have asked permission to conduct his ceremonies wherever it was obviously called for but not wasted his time where it was not. More than likely don Eduardo knew there was no "shaman" in this little village and he did not want to put up with a local bureaucrat's trying to shake us down with some unexpected "fee" for the privilege of staying in their village and walking up the mountain behind it. Whatever happened between them, I'm sure even don Eduardo did not count on the porters not showing up, and it most likely affected him, though how he never said.

The locals did not often make the ascent to the top of the mountain for the very reason we were going there. They knew exactly how it had been used for hundreds of years and they had their own stories about it. But no one remotely anticipated that we would have no porters. I had previously heard claims that don Eduardo did not properly ask permission before bringing a group of Westerners to an ancient site we had visited to conduct our ceremonies. One time I accompanied don Eduardo to visit such a shaman for this very purpose, since the hotel owner had informed us that the premises were under the spiritual protection of such a person. In all honesty, after meeting this shaman both don Eduardo and I found it to be a hollow ritual to earn some money and questionable whether in fact the person before us was much of a shaman. After visiting with us for a short while, he became very apologetic, insisting a mistake had been made and he would never dream of asking us to pay him anything! We invited him to have a beer with us later but never saw him again. A larger feud would escalate into an ugly battle in the months to come. There was a lot of growing jealously among the shamans and sorcerers of Peru regarding don Eduardo; they claimed he had no right to give away "their" knowledge to Westerners.

More than a few scholars in academic circles made claims don Eduardo was Carlos Castaneda's elusive and secretive informant, although this was patently untrue and ironic. A few of us knew don Eduardo believed that Castaneda, through some unknown means, had filched much of don Eduardo's knowledge and teachings into his books and gave the credit to his claimed *nagual* benefactor, don Juan Matus. I don't recall don Eduardo ever bringing up the subject of Castaneda's books but he had read the first two and would discuss them when asked. Don Eduardo insisted that Castaneda's protagonist don Juan was an invented fictional character who definitely did not exist, and yet he would also admit that he knew shamans who possessed the skill and acumen found in Castaneda's books and that he himself was an emissary of some of the very same teachings. Sometimes don Eduardo would fume that Castaneda had reported things ass-backwards and made some things up; other times he almost reverently gave him serious credit for explaining important distinctions very elegantly, even admiring the precision and delicacy.

I was thoroughly familiar with all of Castaneda's writings and enjoyed it immensely whenever don Eduardo would compare and contrast his own experience with anything in those books. It was my destiny to meet and work with the notorious Carlos Castaneda and his family of sorcerers a couple of years later, and possibly the only person to whom Castaneda told the truth outside of his private family. Those tales are for another book, dear friends; first we must understand don Eduardo. At the time I had no personal experience with Carlos Castaneda or his family. The more I realized just how intensely jealous and competitive some in the world of shamans and sorcerers are, the more I could appreciate that the real Don Juan Matus would have a much safer life remaining anonymous if don Eduardo Calderon's life was any measure. The more famous don Eduardo became, no matter how honest or well deserved, the more acrimonious became the reaction in some quarters.

Don Eduardo quipped to me once, "If it's *their knowledge*," referring to other shamans who spoke against him for working with Westerners, "then they would be teaching it just like me. Since they don't have *knowledge*, they can't teach it. That's why people don't come to them."

I believe he was absolutely correct. Real teachers, whether shamans, spiritualists, healers or any real master always serve people with little if any regard to class or race distinctions. It would be impossible, literally impossible, for any real master to approach another human being any other way. Masters do not filter people through their social, class or racial distinctions, though certainly they are aware of them. Masters of any kind simply see who you are, period, and act accordingly. Don Eduardo had become famous when Douglas Sharon wrote a book about him, and later when Shaman Alberto Villoldo, perhaps don Eduardo's most famous apprentice, did as well. And why not? It was all true. He was getting more and more international attention and that just plain bothered a lot of folks. Just how bothered is hard to believe. It's probably the same in any profession. Someone stands out way ahead of the crowd, gets a lot of attention about it, and similar people, whose ideas differ, become resentful and react as though they have been threatened. Jealousy and envy was a big deal in Peru, most certainly among the shamans and the people who revered them, and I would learn more about that firsthand in the months ahead.

As a result of the turf war with the village mayor, we were faced with a challenging situation: three village kids and a couple of camp stoves to heat water and a dwindling supply of tea and food. We respected these young people for defying their elders and making the ascent with us. None of them could take their eyes off the attractive women in our group, and who could blame them? The girl received a lot of gifts and attention from the women in our group, all of which had a deep impact on her life, I'm sure. I had to shake one of the boys out of his wistful trance just to get him to heat water. He was lost in reverie staring at Michelle, who was fully dressed and bending over brushing her teeth fifty yards away. I smiled to myself, mindful of my own appreciation for his feelings, and then handed him matches for the stove.

The girl and one of the boys walked in sandals; the other boy had overly worn street shoes. None of them had adequate clothing for the altitude. They came because they wanted to be in the presence of one of the most famous and powerful shamans in Peru and hoped to receive his blessing. Good for them, we all thought, and holy crap at the same time! What were we going to do for enough nourishment to accomplish what we came to do?

Frankly that question never did get satisfactorily answered so I'll leave it at that.

We all groaned watching Big Beau barking orders at these kids as if his next yell could somehow materialize what was not there to prepare. Once he had inventoried supplies down to the last banana, boxes of corn flakes and jars of whatever, he declared we were in trouble. We all agreed but had very different opinions about what to do. Inevitably, some people raised the idea of going back to the village for supplies but a two-day delay was impossible. We were here, already past "go" and we all realized the play had begun. No stopping it now. So Big Beau started a campaign to send us all out on a food foraging expedition, à la his wilderness tracking school exercises. When he saw our response to his lobbying, it was one of the few times he immediately gave up his agenda. Suddenly it was clear. We would eat what we had brought to eat and do what we came to do. The final day there was no more gas for the stoves, which took forever to light, and we had no hot water.

While still reclining on my granite chair beneath the dazzling starlight within the ceremonial bowl of Marcawasi, my thoughts had revealed a clear and lucid tapestry for how I had come to this very place where I now found myself. It was right that I was there and I was certain about that. Suddenly I was harshly startled out of my reveries and shaken violently into "red alert."

Arrrrooooogaaahhhh!!!   Arrrooogggaaahhhh!!! Arrrooogggaaahhhh!!!

"Gawd almighty what in hell is that sound?" My mind raced to recognize what was going on so I could figure out how to protect myself! The blaring echo around the walls lifted the hair on my arms as if an otherworldly clarion proclaimed the Final Judgment was upon us! For an adrenaline rushed moment I expected aliens to land their spaceship right on top of us as I crouched next to my rock searching for the source of the danger.

Then I let out a deep sigh of amazement! A sense of recognition hit me like an escaped balloon that heaves its last fart. I knew I had been had! In that instant I knew exactly what it was, or at least who it was, although to this day I have no idea how he made that surreal sound. Big Beau was bringing us all to attention. Don Eduardo had emerged from his tent and it was time to gather.

I watched as trails of flashlights around the rim began slowly making their way to the center of the bowl. I bent over and touched my hands to the ground several times, similar to a sprinter before a race, and shook my legs out just like they do. I have no idea why I did that or why I remember except that it indicated how ready I felt. My body was strong and limber and it was affirming to feel that way. My mind and spirit was ready as well, even though I had a slight sense of foreboding at the same time. Just about anything could happen in this group and it would more than likely be well beyond my ability to control, not that I would even dream of doing so, but then what? It was time to find out.

Big Beau barked out an order that reverberated around the entire bowl: "Kill those flashlights!"

He was right. It was utterly unbecoming to walk to a shamanic ceremony with anything except the light of the stars and your own energy body whenever possible, and this night the stars were glorious. The very last thing I wanted to see until the following evening was any kind of artificial light. One by one all the lights went out except a light from one tent, where we could see a clear silhouette moving within.

A distant female voice yelled out, "I'm still finding my tampons, oh gorgeous one. I'll turn it off in a minute."

The powerful yell was squarely directed at Beau, who retorted, "Then get it between your legs or I'll come and help."

"Is that a promise, Honey, or a threat?" came the energized reply while the light went out and she joined us in a circle at the center of the bowl.

We had enjoyed the repartee, including a chuckling don Eduardo. It helped to keep us loose while coming together. He stood before us looking about as magnificent as he had ever done; his presence totally embodied the essence of shaman. Medium height, large-framed and powerfully built, don Eduardo had tawny skin and slightly Asian eyes that indicated his one-quarter Japanese heritage. He wore a long black ponytail. His black and white-striped poncho over a down vest revealed chiseled biceps. He must have known he was on the line and would be tested by the spirits of this place as much as the rest of us. Most of us had many times attended ceremonies with him where wondrous, magical and downright unbelievable things occurred, momentous events that had actually happened and we could attest to it. Fair or not, we all expected don Eduardo to surpass himself, to show us something that took us so far beyond ourselves that we would never get over it.

Seventeen years later I can appreciate the pressure he "might" have felt and the absolute trust and commitment he brought. Around him stood a group of people who had gone to enormous lengths to get there for the sole purpose, at least formally, to receive his blessing as a shaman. Some of his peers were powerfully antagonistic about what he was doing and it must have affected him. He was absolutely sincere about his purpose of making his shamanism available to Westerners. It was his responsibility to make clear to all who would be a shaman, at least acknowledged as such by him, and who was not, and also to minister to everyone's well-being during the process. At the same time he must maintain a fierce purity about the initiation. Otherwise, none of the questions that had brought anyone there could get answered. Only when I weigh all of these factors does what happened that night make sense to me.

What I did not understand until much contemplation years later was that don Eduardo had placed himself at risk at Marcawasi. I don't think he realized just how much until he was there. I think he thought he was so strong that negative forces would leave him alone. Whether or not that's true they certainly did not leave him alone. The old sorcerers who inhabited Marcawasi would come after him several times, and they imparted a psychic uproar among contemporary sorcerers still in physical body, who would try to destroy him in the days to come. Don Eduardo knew his world thoroughly, whereas none of the rest of us did. He must have known, or at least suspected, what was coming. He might have been acting out of sheer nobility, belief in his own destiny, or trusting in *power* and Spirit to carry him through, but ultimately, whatever he believed, he stepped forward and called for the fire to be built.

Big Beau immediately stepped outside our circle to the enormous pile of wood behind him. Several other men joined him and they all brought wood to the center of the circle and smashed it into smaller pieces. Wood splinters shot in all directions while they built a beautiful chest-high teepee of wood. We all stood back and waited to see if don Eduardo would light the fire or call for someone to do it. It was an important distinction whether the shaman entrusted someone to light the fire or whether he felt compelled to do so himself. Either could happen, but whatever the reason and result, it would set the tone and stage for proceeding. Don Eduardo told us the fire should be lit with a match, not a lighter, and waited for someone to step forward.

I had anticipated that moment and stepped forward. Just as I did Beau stepped forward slightly behind me but too late. This action was never as simple as who steps first. It needs to happen seamlessly with a touch of elegance, ritual and drama appropriate to those assembled. Walking up to the wood and striking a match was not the point; the one who chooses to light the fire must first move people and touch them in a way that calls everyone to attention, the right kind of attention. Stepping forward was a personal declaration that you could be counted on to do exactly that, and then you must make it happen.

It was my play, my call. I stepped first and everyone saw it. Then I did not move. I was at ease, and normally I would have walked to the fire and perhaps should have done so. At least that's the expected protocol. The ritual may be the senior value at other places and times, but not here and not now. The raw truth of the moment was my only guide. I did not move. Everyone must have been looking at me but my attention was inside. I recognized that another was supposed to light the fire, and a warm and certain feeling held me still just long enough. In that next moment Kamala and Lorena stepped forward almost from opposite ends of the circle. Virtually in unison, as if on cue, they did not hesitate. They both made a clockwise circle around the wood in front of us and arrived at opposite ends, skillfully lighting matches to the small splinters until they had it going from both sides at the same time. They were both in profile and silhouetted by the fire's light in front of don Eduardo and me. I thought they looked perfectly celestial as if enacting a very ancient ceremony.

Don Eduardo stood directly to my left and once the fire started to ignite, he groaned in a guttural kind of murmuring that was a very typical sound of his during ceremony. Sometimes we could not understand the words but this time they were all too clear. He groused very seriously with a growling kind of edge to it that I should have moved to light the fire. I was completely unprepared to hear his remarks pointedly directed at me. Instantly I felt horrified that I had discredited myself before the ceremony even began. It was an excruciating few moments.

Did I mess this up? started screaming through my head. I had felt so utterly clear and certain. Did don Eduardo specifically mean for me to light the fire? Why? He had never done it that way before and it was not . . . well, normal. I would have done it differently but certainly no better than Lorena and Kamala's beautiful opening.

Then he started joking with me in that same muttering style and I knew it was OK. I exhaled a sigh of relief that was enough to almost blow the fire out fifteen feet away.

"Compadre, your appreciation for the women tricked me," he groused. "Now we will have to rub bellies with the feminine. It will be a strong ceremony for sure."

His tone was joking and ominously serious at the same time. He definitely caught my attention with his emphasis on the feminine. I knew he meant it but I wasn't sure exactly what he meant, although I could tell he was seeing something he preferred to avoid.

Don Eduardo was not at all given to dramatic prognostications beginning ceremonies. He didn't need to! He knew all too well that, "All hell-and hopefully heaven-was gonna break loose" at his San Pedro ceremonies, most especially when it was an initiation fire ceremony, and it would only bring bad luck to say much about it. He was a great deal more disciplined and sophisticated than that, and also an Indian not all that accustomed to being around Westerners, except the last ten years or so. By the time I had met him, don Eduardo had amassed a considerable ability to express himself in almost any situation. He was still a primitive Indian in many ways, however, and I mean that not only positively but also powerfully. He could see through the acquired socialization, which comprised the average person's identity and persona, to a more fundamental recognition of our inherent potential and whether it was activated or dormant within us. Not only shamans but also spiritual masters of every kind perceive in this manner, so while it is a profound level of attainment, it certainly is not unique. The reason it's profound, at least in my opinion, is due to the enormous help don Eduardo could offer. Any serious student dedicated to a spiritual path well knows the rare and powerful experience of finally finding a teacher who recognizes you at a deep level and offers help that affects you very positively. Such persons know the experience of having received a teacher's guidance about something that changed their lives for the better.

Don Eduardo, in his own way, recognized that simply being himself profoundly impacted Westerners, not to say that he was not revered and widely recognized throughout Peru as well. He was a fisherman in his early years and earned his life experience around the docks of Trujillo working as a *curandero,* an indigenous healer, roughly equivalent to a medical doctor with spiritual leanings and trained by one or more people who did the same for the average Indian. Such a person could have any conceivable level of skill and over time their reputation would reflect their level of ability. A *curandero* might be a neighbor woman to consult for colds and childbirth, or a certain farmer for injuries and bone setting in the fields, but neither would be regarded as more than just a person who can help in minor medical emergencies. A larger notoriety had to be earned and demonstrated over time before the public could believe it, not unlike most every other walk of life. Not every *curandero* would be considered a medicine man: someone remarkably skilled at using herbs and spiritual energy to heal and affect human events, let alone as a shaman venerated for spiritual mastery.

As a young man don Eduardo had traveled extensively to work with the great shamans of his day in Peru, which is how one learns the craft, and the government frequently consulted him about antiquities excavated from digs. People who watch a shaman and come to their ceremonies (or not) tell others. A shaman's identity and reputation is all word-of-mouth and person-to-person, at least before Westerners came along and started writing books. He had traveled to Japan for training in Oriental perspectives and sometimes the Japanese came to attend his ceremonies. He was widely known and recognized, mostly by the average person in Peru.

When walking with don Eduardo around the streets of Cuzco, sometimes people would quickly walk up to him with their head bowed or kneel in front of him. "Don Eduardo, please forgive me a moment of your time. Please bless me on my way to work. I left a sick child home and my wife. . ."

Don Eduardo would simply pause and if he were smoking his pipe at the time, he would bless that person with strong currents of shaman plasma-enriched smoke blown fiercely across the brow and heart. Believe me, when don Eduardo did this to you it felt great! Or he might grab the person's head if he did not have his pipe out, and strongly or gingerly rub their forehead or the top of their head and chant a blessing over them. All this would happen almost perfunctorily, automatically, quickly, and always with an air of dignity.

I never forgot a certain incident with don Eduardo while we were walking down a narrow cobble street in Cuzco. A pathetic, emaciated and very desperate looking man had quickly rushed up and placed his face on don Eduardo's boots while wailing about his situation. Don Eduardo pretty much grabbed him by the scruff of his neck and lifted him straight up. Holding him by the shoulder in a powerful one-hand grip he "smoked him" while sternly telling him to get his life together and stop acting like a bum. Then he released him affectionately with some encouraging remarks to go and find a restaurant and wash dishes for his dinner, and we walked on.

When don Eduardo noticed my reaction he spoke to me very sharply.

"He was beaten down without the added weight of your eyes on his back. Your disrespect for the Indians must be corrected, even though I know you do not mean to be that way."

At first I was stunned. I stammered, "I would never intentionally be disrespectful and I can't understand why you would say that." I probably started to get really defensive since I had no clue what I had done.

You looked at him with pity," he said pointblank. "Your pity for the Indians will only kill them and they will hate you for it. I trust you will see it more clearly from here."

I have always been clear about it since. I felt intensely embarrassed in that moment and I must have looked like it.

"No need for that, my friend," he said as if taking stock of my reaction as he placed his hand on my shoulder. "Shamans learn from their mistakes instead of looking back. You will have plenty more chances to greet us (Indians) with dignity, I assure you."

The raw, unexpected unfolding of what happens for people at a San Pedro ceremony is the glorious wild card that every shaman must bow to with respect and courage. The shaman enacts what has been given to him from years of practice. The basic ceremonies are fixed with certain structures, and yet what happens can only be predicted up to a certain point. There's a joke we all have heard that whiskey (or pick your alcohol) brings out the real person. I have never seen that to be true, although I have seen my share of amazing intoxicated performances and given a few myself. With the unique effects of San Pedro cactus ceremoniously prepared by native Andean Shamans, however, it's an entirely different level of intoxication with zero resemblance to alcohol or just about anything else.

The traditions of the Indians from every part of North and South America, who use a mescaline psychoactive cactus integral to their spiritual heritage, all say some very consistent and reverent things about it. *The Teacher* is a term and concept I believe is found in every indigenous culture whose shamans have a relationship with *mescalito* through the cactus. While one particular native community might overtly relate to *The Teacher* in the form of a magical deer, another in the form of spiritual ancestors, another in the form of abstract entities that communicate, all address this level of contact with profound respect and gratitude. Even our own great literary exponents of the "mescaline journey" arrive at a similar place, such as in Aldous Huxley's *Doors of Perception*, where he provides a narration of his mind expansion and what the mescaline-induced journey "taught" him. Not the same for the shaman, however. For the shaman, *The Teacher* is not his own mind or the cactus itself, which he regards as a "botanical medicine" that activates normally innate channels in the human psyche, and with proper training most especially the capacity to interact with alternate levels of reality that can bring value and blessing to our everyday experience. When the shaman finally learns to navigate the cactus medicine provides transportation to a *being* that lives within a reality matrix intersected by the cactus plant. That *being* is *The Teacher mescalito*, a real entity at least as real as you and me, and shamans have very good reason to report their experience in this manner.

Whenever don Eduardo intoned anything with or without an ominous note, I learned to take him literally, not because anything bad happened, rather because something always occurred that he referenced back to what he had said. He wanted me to learn how to read things coming, so to speak, but it usually turned out he meant something very different than what I had expected. While Kamala and Lorena lit the fire, his words were having an effect on me but I was not certain how. There had been a few times when don Eduardo referred to female shamans and feminine force with very real trepidation, so I was not totally surprised hearing these kinds of remarks from him. But then we never talked about these or any other subjects while beginning a ceremony. I knew his experience and attitude toward women and the feminine were complex, to say the least.

I did not look to don Eduardo to provide my values and never felt obliged to share his view of the social order. Those who did were constantly trying to reconcile contradictions, at least it seemed to me. I was in Peru to learn shamanism and that was more than difficult by itself. Judging don Eduardo's life through my interpretations would have made it impossible. I related to don Eduardo as the shaman inheritor of an ancient sacred craft and I felt privileged to share many kinds of moments with him. I never changed my stance about that and never went out of my way to learn anything about don Eduardo's life that he did not place in front of me, but none of this was a simple or easy stance since it was inevitable and natural that he was talked about a great deal. I looked out and saw Lorena and Kamala in perfect profile and it looked entirely right to me that they were lighting the fire.

Then the shaman continued the ceremony. There is no way I can convey in the written medium the feelings evoked from don Eduardo whistling and singing and rattling and the effect it would have. Listening to a recording of his ceremonial chanting will give some sense of understanding, but essentially I'm saying that the effect was profound, joyful, mesmerizing, enchanting and utterly compelling. Don Eduardo was a virtuoso, not a performer, rather he was a master whose sounds and rhythms and movements were totally commanding. If one knew nothing about *power* or even shamanism, participating in a San Pedro ceremony with Shaman don Eduardo Calderon, no matter who you were, left a deep mark in the psyche. His presence alone, before we had even opened the flask to his wondrous elixir, was a rarefied intoxication that people like our group had waited our entire lives to bear witness to. On this occasion most especially, the focus, intention and execution went beyond what was already extraordinary.

First the shaman opens the ceremony with a dramatic call to the Winds of the Four Directions and for this don Eduardo had become famous. Every North or South American shaman works with the cardinal directions in one way or another, and it's something the people recognize. However the shaman conducts his ceremony, touching those present is the whole point. Don Eduardo is not a performer, although obviously in a certain sense he is. More accurately he is a trance master. Every iota of his being is taking us into as deep a different reality as we are capable of and willing to enter.

His call sent waves of feelings through us. At times like these the Winds must answer and the Shaman proves his stuff. Stepping forward, lifting his Tibetan bells above his head, the sound reverberated around the canyon walls in an eerie symphony of subtle echoes coming from every direction and tapping everyone's energy body. A few people jerked with the kind of twitch that comes from being hit with a shocking dose of energy. All of us were suddenly standing an inch or two taller.

71

Next came an eloquent series of chants to all of don Eduardo's teachers. He called them out by name one by one, sending his gratitude into the stars whose shimmer said they were listening. A wind blew first in one direction across the fire, and then in another direction while it was growing in size, except none of us felt any wind. One at a time don Eduardo faced the Winds of the Four Directions, striking the bells, blowing his magical perfume in powerful bursts of "swoosh" that engulfed our senses with aromatic impact. He formally addressed the spirit essence of each of the directions with a heartfelt personal intensity as though something invisible was right there in front of him. Again the fire blew one way, and then another way with enough rush across the flames that they could be heard as well as seen, yet none of us felt any wind, at least not the physical kind. Though none of us yet saw what he so passionately addressed we all felt we stood before the same presence. Except for the flames, at times the air was totally still and empty and had been since late afternoon and still the fire whooshed as though an invisible billows moved around it.

After calling out each of the Four Winds, followed by personally addressing the power animals of each and beseeching them to bestow their gifts upon us, don Eduardo worked to transform the fire, to entice it to become friendly, to become an energetically spiritual portal into other dimensions. He respectfully and formally requested, sometimes demanded, other times "sweet talked" and beseeched the fire to serve us and not burn, that it purify and not scorch, and above all that it heal and offer visions and energy to fulfill our purposes. Time drifted away as don Eduardo worked on the fire, taking a staff from his mesa that he had laid next to me, then a sword, then another sword. Many times he reached and thrust into the fire with magical passes to entice the fire to transform into something more than flames and burning wood. Sometimes he kneeled in front of the fire and blew one of his oils across it making a huge flame, other times he blew his pipe smoke with enough force to make the fire puff like a giant mushroom, then he moved around the fire again, chanting, singing, whistling, while his sounds became a strange symphony reverberating around us.

As the fire grew, it lit up the entire bowl with eerie towering forms of light and dark shadows moving all around the walls, dancing to our sounds and looming over our shoulders. This was not the first time I had stood with shamans in ceremony that called "the ghosts to come and witness," a most unfortunate term but the one often used. It was a generic term referring to anything that was alive but not organic that our ceremonies attracted both intentionally and serendipitously. It was taught to me that the *power* of the shaman must include enough strength and skill to "keep them in the peanut gallery." That's a term I made up to convey exactly what the shaman means. Since the very nature of shamanic ceremonies is to bring light into the darkness, many levels of sentient life forms come like moths to warm themselves at the real and metaphorical fire, the light of the mesa and San Pedro ceremonies. Essentially the shaman stands as a living embodiment of the human blessing to all life forms and shamans conducting ceremonies in the wild actively communicate with non-human sentience for many purposes. Opening and closing ceremonies for shamans all over the world often include blessings to inorganic cohabiting life forms upon our planet and in our universe. *Blessing them and knowing they are there is one thing, attempting to purposely interact with them is quite another.* Not all shamans directly concern themselves and prefer instead to simply acknowledge their presence and seek nothing further. Don Eduardo's tradition was different. He was a man willing to demonstrate everything taught from his oral medicine wheel tradition, but none of us had ever heard anything about giant shadows dancing like human forms and participating with us around our circle.

Don Eduardo's training was to keep our attention on the flow of the ceremony and most especially on whatever the shaman was doing. We learned to be aware of whatever comes around us, but never to allow it to affect or change the flow of what the ceremony was about. Not an idle exercise! To actually fulfill that instruction at times like these required enormous internal discipline. According to the shaman, his strength combined with the integrity of the participants obliged any "ghostly or ethereal" visitors to "only watch." The shaman's teaching lineage passed to me orally claimed that no entity could crack the power of the circle during "a properly conducted San Pedro ceremony." In practice don Eduardo's teaching was seldom that simple or easy.

We all wanted to believe that we were safe within our circle and ceremony from intrusion but in practice it did not always work out that cleanly. I had seen many people interfered with by visiting entities and when this happens, the shaman immediately moves to protect them if he was not already moving to head the entity off. In my experience, most people, and I mean most, are not psychologically or spiritually well equipped for contact with other life forms. Combined with the effects of the San Pedro, it usually turns people into a basket case requiring help. That's the learning curve for the modest public who find their way into these esoteric ceremonies. It can be a royal pain in the ass to go to great lengths to arrive at a ceremony with a real shaman in extraordinary circumstances only to have another participant become an unruly and undisciplined case. In this particular circle of substantial beings, I had no concerns in this regard. I knew, respected and trusted everyone to maintain our circle, no matter what.

Rationally, I knew the forms were shadows from the fire, but none of us had ever, I mean *ever*, seen shadows like these. Many times they became alive and were half the size of the huge wall and they would lean down with enormous peering necks and extend their shadowy plasma very close to our circle. It was beyond weird, even spooky, and yet I was profoundly grateful for every moment. Even though we had just begun, I was already reaching feelings and sensibilities and levels of awareness that made everything I came for seem complete. Just being there was more than enough.

We became increasingly entranced into a fantastic reverie, when suddenly, completely catching me off-guard, don Eduardo abruptly stopped his singing and sat down. An immediate silence fell across the circle except for the crackling fire. The fire brightly lit our faces, allowing all of us to take sober notice of where we were and what we were doing. Don Eduardo's ceremonial timing exquisitely played with the silence that would loudly dominate our feelings at times. We noticed more and more figures taking form on the enormous walls around us as the fire grew. Later in the evening one particular football-shaped face with a giraffe-like elongated neck, which was about ninety feet high, careened from a towering location two hundred feet above us. Time and again it would lift itself off the wall and lean face down onto the top of our circle as if it wanted a close-up look at us. Imagine looking up at such a thing looking down at you. I saw intense curiosity bordering on enjoyment coming from this being and nothing menacing. Finally one of the shapes would completely leap from the wall and step autonomously onto the bowl floor, requiring the shaman's full participation in cosmic drama *par excellence*.

Sitting on his mesa, don Eduardo took his bottle of perfumes and essences that he called his "insurance." Whoooosh several times, then again with the pipe, as he blessed and prayed over the flask of *white lightning*, his private mixture of San Pedro, the psychotropic cactus of the Andes revered by shamans for thousands of years. He uncorked the top and blew into its contents. His prayers now became incantations and holy salutes to an ancient source of *power* for don Eduardo and countless Peruvian shamans, the inter-dimensional ally known as *mescalito*. The flask contained the *white lightning*, a distilled and extraordinarily concentrated mixture made from the San Pedro cactus. This was don Eduardo's private mixture, selected from a secret location where certain cacti grew tended by a continuous family lineage for hundreds of years. No one I had ever met who knew anything about San Pedro ever disputed that don Eduardo's mixture was the best of the best in a class by itself and this night most especially.

First, don Eduardo poured the mixture into a shot glass and after blessing it many times he drank it down in a single swig. I was sitting next to him on his right and he told me to stand and approach the mesa. I accepted the glass from him while he continued his incantations and drank it down in a single gulp; it was a wonderfully tasty material with the hint of anisette. Then every person came to the mesa one at a time and he handed each of us a shot glass of *white lightning,* the corridor of potential to the higher realms, the ecstasy of the shaman we all prayed for in one way or another. We lifted our glasses toward the stars, internally stated our intention for being there, then drank it down in a single gulp and stamped our foot hard on the ground while whistling into the emptied glass and saluting the heavens with the sound "mescalito" bursting from our lips as though we meant to blow against a star. As each person made their way around the circle, their unique walk, presence and energy were all there, fully visible. Progressively through the night we became more and more transparent to each other, lucidly sharing transpersonal dimensions and every other kind of dimension as well.

Once we had all consumed a shot glass of the *white lighting* before the mesa, Shaman don Eduardo immediately began to chant and whistle and sing with his commanding and utterly mesmerizing rattling. Many, if not all of us, had drums and rattles and other instruments and we lit that entire bowl with a sound that increased and expanded in volume and tapestry and complexity while those figures danced and weaved on the undulating walls around us. We were at least eight-thousand-foot elevation higher than any of us had ever been to do medicine work before, and if that had any affect on us that night it was profound. I personally call it *high holy adventure*. The *white lightning* works in stages, and takes you to three thresholds, each more intense than the last. When you could not believe that anything more intense was possible, it would increase and increase until nothing, nothing was the same. Whatever I write from here is a pale re-creation of a memory of what cannot easily be told.

Don Eduardo was no longer only a person. In one moment he was a commanding Indian performing breathtaking moves and emitting sounds that were more animal and etheric than human and in the very same moment he was not a person as much as he was energetic figures and shapes and forms. Energy-like beings moved in and out of the same space his body occupied. He could be a horse or a jaguar prowling, then disappear completely into amorphous energy that became a mirror into your own lucid consciousness. Then I was traveling deeply within, no longer even aware if my eyes were open or closed since either way I perceived the same thing. Normal recognition and ninety percent of my cognitive world dropped away. An utterly lucid, commanding and engulfing presence swallowed my mind, my psyche and my body and I found myself inhabiting another reality entirely. What used to be one hundred percent of myself was now only ten percent and was within a vast multidimensional field of awareness and perception that became my newfound ninety percent self recognition.

Some part of me peered across the fire at the canyon wall in the distance. My vision telescoped to the millimeter level and looked at a tiny insect moving on the wall. Then the wall undulated as if it felt me inspecting it so closely that it tickled. My vision involuntarily receded until I was looking at the entire rim of the bowl, 360 degrees around me at the same time with a point of view about a mile higher than my body. Then I was looking at everyone in our circle except I did not see only a person. Everyone was porous and fluid as much as a solid form, sometimes visible as people and sometimes only recognizable as pools of energy changing form. Gazing at anyone was sheer communication. Our normally "personal" consciousness was no longer recessed behind the appearance of our body. Each of us was a total visual feeling and energetic presence fully revealed, right there *to see*.

One of the men in our group, Stefan, got up and began to circle the fire as though he was an animal prowling a friendly environment. Our drumming and chanting were even louder and no musicians anywhere could provide a more perfect sonic tapestry for our drama. He leaped out in front of himself as though he was a giant bullfrog trailing tendrils of light. He landed with a

77

frog-like plop and then exploded into various serendipitous dance movements that resembled a swimmer in water more than a body moving on land. Several times he moved around the circle until he thrust himself into a spread kneeling position immediately in front of the fire. There were trails of light streaming from his graceful movements as he waved his hands over the fire, inviting the flames to brush against him. Soon he pulled open his shirt and with his hands he drew smoke from the lower embers, pulling it again and again toward his belly, then toward his heart, then toward his head and down over his body, cleansing and purifying himself with the smoke. His movements were his prayers and the smoke became holy incense delivered from his moments before the fire. He gratefully accepted the smoke to cleanse and heal his energy body and to restore, replenish and empower his life.

This beautiful man, Stefan, was a Swiss international discharged from the Army for snoring, who made the peaks of the Andes sit up and listen, and unfortunately the rest of the camp as well. Before the fire he continued to pour out soulful movements that drew all of our attention. We were there with him, at the fire and most emphatically at his back with our protection against anything external that might tap him at such vulnerable moments. At a fire ceremony it's necessary that the person at the fire display enough authentic presence to legitimately draw everyone's full attention. Sounds simple, which it is, but also very demanding and very serious although it's entirely up to the person at the fire what that may look like.

During a fire ceremony, it is the duty of the participants to give full and undivided attention to the person before the fire *without interfering*, and also *to protect them*. It is believed that the person before the fire must be vulnerable enough to let go of their social persona, personality structure, need to please and being pleased, or any other agenda at any level *and simply let go to the truth of the moment.* Giving your full and undivided attention for twenty plus people would be demanding under any circumstances but to maintain such a state of unified vigilance was both impossible and vitally necessary. Giving anything your full and undivided attention to anything external could become incomprehensible and yet a recognizable coherence and order to our ceremony had to be maintained. How? There was nothing left of linear thinking to pay attention with. And yet it did flow in a kind of natural unfolding, which had everything to do with the *power* of the shaman to generate a unified reality that pulled at everyone with an overwhelming invitation to arrive at the same intersection. The shaman never forces anyone into anything. Instead, he invites with such an intoxicating allure that he cannot be refused. One's ability to accept his invitation has a great deal to do with readiness to hold the space being offered.

The ceremony turns around a state of being orchestrated by the shaman and what everyone personally brings to these moments. The movements and rituals are all pro forma decoration, truthfully, and the real meat and potatoes is always and only what each of us uniquely bring forth from a place within that is true, authentic unfiltered presence without any personality agenda and yet graceful, powerful, and contributing to the whole. Any time anyone *can be* that inner truth, everyone is profoundly served and all are grateful. The fire ceremony is only the external structure and is brought forward from the mists of our origins. The ceremony provides the time and place and means to let go, to make contact within the *nagual*, to experience *power* and most importantly experience that always leads to the Light of Love. What else is there, ultimately? Shamans, real shamans, master shamans absolutely know it's about love and confirm it again and again through these ceremonies. Sharing their *knowledge* is for us the high road to heaven, *high holy adventure*.

The purpose of the fire ceremony is to have a moment before the fire that transforms you. When done properly, not only the shaman but also often everyone else can *see* into your heart, share your wisdom for being there, understand your injury or wound and what you are choosing to do about that, and many other deep, inner personal matters. Having that holy and "private" moment in full view of everyone and everything in this circle of people and stone means hiding nothing. At this point you are talking directly to The Spirit from a place inside you that absolutely means it.

Over time and many fire ceremonies, participants learn the only guarantee not to disgrace oneself, either from holding back and being inauthentic, or letting go like a fool without internal focus, is to live a disciplined life, an authentic life, a life congruent to one's own ideals, whatever they may be. What comes out at the fire ceremony is who we truly are. At least that's the premise of the shamans as it was given to me through don Eduardo. We go to the fire to learn who we are becoming, and then to enter into ourselves as fully as the fire ceremony and the next day and year will allow.

When one goes before the fire like this, the shaman who is working on many channels can see many things about you. He can often see what you may or may not know about yourself. Not always what you have had for breakfast, but literally who you are being at the fire. Who and what are you manifesting? Are you guided by The Spirit or portraying your ego? Is your vision wide-ranging in focus or myopic? Is your life disciplined or boring? Is your compassion awake, is your mind clear, are your relationships vital, are you holding onto something miserably weak, an old story you have not let go? The shaman never judges any of it if only because he can't *see* any of this from a place of judgment. From his place of ecstatic detachment *he only sees whoever is before him at the fire* and acts accordingly. He may later call you before his mesa to work with your energy body to help you in some way or to send you energy in the circle.

Eventually our first pilgrim sprang to his feet, complete with the fire, and danced back to his place in the circle. Everyone was peacefully and kindly touched by his exchange with the fire. The *white lightning* expanded again, coursing like rushing bursts, imploding and exploding within and without. Several people took their time before the fire, each in a unique and spontaneously expressed choreography with The Spirit. The opening and the penetration into non-ordinary reality continued to increase and deepen. The moves at the fire were personal and serious and intended to manifest our intent, whatever we had said in our deepest truth that we meant to call forth from that fire, that magical portal that don Eduardo held open through the flames. The first half dozen people to go before the fire were all lovely souls who showed us gentleness, their humanity, their humility, their wounds, which they presented for healing, and their dignity in being there. Their movements were open, honest, strong and sincere and above all utterly spectacular in their beauty. Not in the normal sense of "judging" anything they did as beautiful, rather from sheer witnessing of being. It was all pure and natural, with enough discipline and focus to allow letting go with full intention.

Without trying at first I spontaneously watched whether any item on don Eduardo's mesa would light up when a person was before the fire. He had a hundred or so objects on his mesa and each one delivered a single distinct message to reveal something to him about that person. One object might tell him the health of someone's liver, another whether their wife or husband was having an affair, another if they were in danger from black magic, another to locate something they had lost. Usually when a power object lit up from someone's presence, don Eduardo would work on him or her later in the ceremony per the particular object's message, but not this night. Soon the medicine expanded so ferociously that I had no consciousness left that could concern itself with don Eduardo's mesa. I never returned to that level of concrete consciousness the rest of the night, not to say power objects are "concrete." This *white lightning medicine* was closing off our awareness of anything recognized or rehearsed to enter the playing field now before us.

Expanding, expanding, engulfing, enveloping feelings, feelings made of light and sounds and energy transforming who and what I was. Strength, tremendous well-being, no sense of personality ego or identity-self, only raw sheer willingness to fulfill intentions for being there. No longer "my" intentions. Only intentions. Underneath the veneer of personal identification and self-reflecting head talk was an operational level of identity where another me resided, and according to these feelings proclaimed liberation. What was left after ego persona ceases to exist? Fierce determination. Hold. Let go. Hold. Let go. Hold and let go. Hold "the mind" to intention and let go into this enormous expansion. Deeper, deeper, lucidly brilliant colors, patterns, forms fluidly changing and shifting. I was no longer a person or a body. Nothing was a "thing" while everyone was energy and flow. Sheer intent was the orienting self now. My deepest intentions guided or manifested my consciousness. I no longer inhabited a privately personal space. Someone else, a deeper me, a real me became a functioning and fully operational "me." I was totally clear that I existed as part of . . . The Spirit. THE INFINITELY LOVING WHOLE. The Source. Infinite vastness and yet I was the very fabric of the eternal. A pure and unfiltered-by-thought level of experiential recognition affirmed this. I was not thinking about . . . anything; I was engulfed in *direct experience that required nothing else*. I recognized "my" existence as a fluid texture of awareness, energy and consciousness within a fabric of ultimate reality of which I was a part. I belonged to the created and the Creator at the same time.

Then I was standing up without any awareness of doing so. I had no volition about movement and I was not local to my body. My self-location and perspective shifted fluidly from one moment to the next. I was aware of intense well-being while feeling a power moving through my body although I could not easily locate "me" in my body or even care. I was an abstract relationship to my body rather than being an entity within it. I was an abstract thought guiding my body through intent without any thinking about it. *Mescalito* had turned on my deep automatic pilot and someone else, at least another level of me not easily contacted, was now fully operational and present.

With a flourish, I leaped from where I stood snatching one of don Eduardo's mesa swords as I rushed clockwise into the circle. The shaman energetically erupted by blowing enormous clouds of fragrance over me with such explosive energy that I reeled head over heels backwards as if intentionally exercising a full roll, responding to Eduardo's cloudburst, arriving on my feet in front of the fire with the sword pointing upright. Then crouching and circling the fire, I made passes to the directions through the flames as they whished and whooshed this way and that way and all I could realize was a rapturous state moving me while I saw light and energy as much as I perceived flames. My movements were almost compulsive acts from a desire ignited from within to touch and be touched by what I saw. The flame would vanish into a nothingness that emitted something gold and blue that was pulling me toward it with an irresistible allure of love with such personal recognition as though family were calling me from home. Finally kneeling before the fire and facing the North, I planted the sword deliberately as I stared into the flames.

Prayer, deep prayer, what was my purpose here, what was I doing here? What did I want? What was my intent now, right then? Intent, come forward. Tell me why I am here. Relationship. The Spirit. The Light of Love. The eternal relationship that my being proclaims as true, real, and forever. The Spirit and the light of love were what I saw "out there" from the same place in me that was one and the same. That profoundly gold and blue flame radiating eternal love heralded authority from the universe where no doubt was possible. Loving profound authority in sinewy golden blue light. Eternal safety and wholeness was all that it radiated.

"I want only You," I cried aloud to The Spirit and the loving warmth called to me, although I didn't know if my external voice was involved.

In that moment I affirmed something that came from my heart and the core of my being. It just came out. I did not claim, nor was I aware of any thoughts relating to shamanism, nor was any other cognitive train of thinking present.

"YOU are my path," I cried to The Spiritual Love I felt before me, "the Home I have never left." I spoke into that portal of brilliant energy, although at a much deeper and precognitive level of experience than words easily convey.

Without any semblance of normal awareness or any self-reflection, I placed my hands into the middle of the golden blue flames while I prayed, and prayed and prayed. It was not the flames that I reached out to touch, however, rather it was into the center of this luminous opening with sheets of radiance pouring out such loveliness that it was impossible not to reach out and touch it. I was touching a feeling of profound love that offered me my innocence beyond any level of sentimental tears. Touching that radiance was to feel and to know that everything was safe, that all was well, that it never could be any other way. I cannot truly write the experience, yet words can direct attention to what we may know within ourselves.

"You are my Source," I said to the loving feeling and Spirit Light.

It was an exalted state of being that was timeless and seamless and touching that golden sweet radiance was all that I felt. I have no way of knowing how long in time because I was no longer aware of anything except an utterly abstract state of being.

Then, as if someone had walked up behind me, a voice demanded in my ear, "What do you want?" The voice was harsh and loud and clear, in a manner that was completely incongruent with my state of being. I was utterly shocked, and forced into realizing I was kneeling before a fire in front of a circle during a ceremony at Marcawasi and the impossible had just occurred.

It was NOT the voice of The Spirit, nor was it from anyone in the circle; no one could talk, let alone be heard over our chanting and drumming. The voice instantly changed my state of attention. Was it a psychic communication from the old world sorcery of this place? Was it the voice of *mescalito*? Was it something else? Should I answer?

"What do you want?" the voice spoke again in a sharp and more demanding tone.

"I come *from* Love," something in me instantly replied.

"Then you have come to the wrong place," the voice said with an air of contempt and challenge.

84

A part of me recognized that I was wide open and exposed at the fire and that more than our circle was peering into my psychic space. Another sentience was listening to my inner world on loudspeaker and was personally responding as if with authority to challenge me. I responded to the voice one more time, except telling it like a dialogue mistranslates what was more abstract. In my mind's eye I *saw power* and *Love* as one and the same thing, and I emoted that thought image realization to the voice with an outpouring of feelings.

"Very well then," the booming voice replied without accepting or rejecting my communication. The tone was like a judge pronouncing an order from the bench.

Without trying, my vision adjusted and I looked straight ahead to see Big Beau's eyes meeting mine except Big Beau was not exactly himself either. The dim yellow and green glisten over his eyes was prominent until his face turned into non-recognizable swirling energy; then his face would return only to be gone again. It was the same whenever I looked at anyone, visually perceiving energy that conveyed intense feelings from holy to ecstatic, to rapturous, to struggle and challenge and whatever that person's core state of being emitted. Seeing anyone in that state conveyed intense and distinct feelings and spontaneous information on many levels of awareness. Looking at Big Beau was like watching Robinson Crusoe surviving on his little island while remaining oblivious to the modern cruise ships landing nearby. He was a stand-alone spiritual warrior in our midst, at least he thought so, and gripped entirely by something powerful and archaic. He was looking deeply into me now and I was looking right back into him. I saw his fundamental state of being as clearly as I perceived anyone else, also his genuine concern for many things both noble and dark, and his seriousness underneath all that bizarre discipline, and he knew that I was peering deeply into his personal space.

Then my vision *almost* returned to normal when I saw that my hands were still in the blue flames. The normal me was not present because I had no reaction to it. They were just there, even though I realized they were in flames. Slowly and steadily I looked into Beau's yellowish slit eyes, thin sheets of green veneer extruded sideways from his brow as I reached down into the flames and lifted one of the burning logs and laid it on its side. Then I stood up, or more exactly I became aware that I was standing without knowing how I did it. Something naturally directed my eyes to Kamala except she too was changed. She now looked like I had always perceived her to be, a temple priestess of the highest order wearing a purplish crescent of energy like a tiara over her head. Her energy was radiant and her eyes were shining from another dimension like the stars peering from infinity into mine.

One by one we each found our turn and place at the fire. Most everyone was beautiful in some respect and everyone became exceptionally transparent, at least to many of us. It was pure witnessing of being and often a person's issues and relationships would appear on their shoulders as they knelt before the fire. Even though the process is a long one, by the time everyone had gone to the fire the *white lightning* was still expanding. On a practical note, none of us had ever experienced a medicine as powerful. That was exceptional, especially among this very experienced group.

After we had all gone to the fire and our drumming had softened, Shaman don Eduardo got to his feet to work on our energy bodies, loosely referred to as *cleansing, or "getting powdered."* Essentially, the shaman performs a sequence of magical passes using a rattle to strike our bodies in order to take care of whatever he *saw* about us that needed his energetic help. This ritual is the shaman's gift from his ecstatic trance to cleanse and strengthen our energy bodies most especially. Anyone can perform the gestures but not just anyone can make them work. When don Eduardo worked on us in these ceremonies, we were literally being touched by a transpersonal lineage of shamans that reached from the beginning through the ecstatic shaman now hitting us with his rattle. And we felt his touch on many levels.

"Wap, wap, wap, humma humma humma" his rattle would strike our body done in the same way for who can say how long while he voiced lyrical cadences and guttural rolls and trills to his chants? Invariably we would feel much, much more than the rattle's gentle touch: true inter-dimensional contact could be a way of saying what it felt like. Don Eduardo was not don Eduardo; he was Shaman, a continuous being for twenty-five thousand years, who was reaching into our ceremonial circle through the fire to embrace each of us. The embodiment of something trans-dimensional, a consciousness co-habiting the shaman's body and mind without don Eduardo losing himself. The shaman is different than the spiritualist medium who will entirely give away his mind and body for another spirit to occupy. The shaman will always retain a portion of his own self-referencing identity; the ten percent, always enough to witness whatever influences or creates his existence. A shaman, according to don Eduardo, will never allow total immersion from another spirit entity into his own constitution so that personal identity no longer exists. At some level the shaman always knows who he is and insists he will maintain his self-reference *all the way home*.

Don Eduardo had already energetically cleansed several people when I first noticed it. A shadow was no longer dancing on the far wall from the firelight and had instead rushed into our circle, literally hovering over don Eduardo's back. The hovering was purposefully menacing and close enough to press him with an ominous challenge. Kamala, the Roshi, Lorena and Beau, a lot of us saw it at the same time. We had been witnessing these bizarre and outlandish shadows and must have assumed there was some kind of safety within our circle; at least I doubt anyone ever expected a shadow to leave the walls. Even the leaning face from above always remained above our circle and attached to the high wall. Now the close appearance of this black plasma kite had dissipated any sense of separation between our circle and the forces around us. Every sentient and alive entity and force that was a part of this gigantic bowl was now attending our ceremony. My feelings of rapturous abandon shifted to a strange kind of warrior protective vigilance added to an acute awareness of the many levels of life forms that surrounded us.

Don Eduardo suddenly whirled around and grabbed his tall staff from the mesa. He sliced through the air hurling powerful screams at this incandescently dark amorphous mass jutting over and around his head like a fantastic hang- glider-size bat that would not go away. This utterly surreal, bizarre scene unfolding in front of us had overtones of a cosmic conspiracy between two tricksters intent on shaking us out of any final vestiges of normal reality. At one point the kite being acted like it wanted to slice through don Eduardo's guts and serve him for dinner. We felt its ferocious hunger lapping at our feet and had there been any place to run for cover it would have been tempting, yet we all held our place. Then don Eduardo's *powers*, his jaguar energy most especially, would launch a furious attack into the dark plasma with enough vengeance to drive it back to Hades. In some manner we had to breathe and try to calm down because we were on the edge of sanity watching this play out!

There are levels of tension that one simply cannot approach or the risk of escape without damage becomes too great. At the edge of the tension a lustful sweetness would inexplicably be evoked and somehow soothe the nerves enough for us to remain present. The entire scene would abruptly shift and don Eduardo, the seducer, looked like he could be chasing the most delicious intimate encounter imaginable while "she" was coyly egging him forward. We could almost be dripping love juices from vicariously watching . . . what? What were we watching? How on earth were we sensing and feeling a spectacle so utterly outside the set of anything easily imaginable? We were inside out, with our feelings telling us what we saw, and our eyes filling it in. We were fully present though nowhere recognizable. We were left to accept or not what was happening right in front of our faces. *They* were creating a dance that made love with a ferociously embattled energy they both embraced. It was then I understood. The dark energy was feminine, a female sorcerer and/or her dark plasma projection, the last thing don Eduardo said that he had ever wanted to deal with. Or so he claimed. On the one hand it meant that he had brought enough personal power to attract "her" interest, on the other hand don Eduardo did not want the fight since he thought very few male shamans could survive one.

So this encounter was proof of don Eduardo's tension about the feminine omens all along, or at least a part of it, which he confirmed the next day. Perhaps this was the truth behind the mythos of Homer's Ulysses tying himself to the mast while his ship sailed within earshot of the siren's enchantment. The allure is too great and only death waits for the would be warrior lover. Whether clever like Ulysses I can't say, but this was what don Eduardo did. After this utterly fantastic staff kata of chasing this hovering kite plasma around the fire appearing to almost make love with her in swooning movements, or banishing her into the cinders with other movements, she finally expanded and receded onto the walls and it was done. Not only with this entity but also with the entire entity presence around us. They would no longer interfere or challenge our movements the rest of that night, and somehow this was understood throughout the bowl. My sense of red alert about life forms in the bowl with us completely relaxed. The dance was complete and not a word or sound except for the fire was heard. Don Eduardo placed two crisscrossed swords behind the mesa where he sat to signal his personal energy remained active at the mesa. Then he performed a brief salute to the directions in such a way as to let us all know that the "fire ceremony remained open," an obvious fact to all of us since the intensity of the experience was still expanding. Even if the shaman was done with the circle, no one was close to being finished with the ceremony and we all knew it.

Without saying a word, don Eduardo looked me square in the eyes from another world, walked past me out of the circle and went back to his tent, leaving the ceremony still wide open. No preamble, no explanation, as if anyone could talk at such a time anyway. He was just gone. We all stood there watching the fire burning and crackling. The *white lightning* was still cresting. We stood motionless for quite a while, automatically anticipating that he might return. We had no idea or any cognitive ability at the time to assess the matter. Energy and intent and deeper purposes were orchestrating everything. Don Eduardo had been overwhelmed at ceremony a couple of times previously from deliberately sucking off ugly energy from people who needed it. At those times, before he stepped out of the circle, he would grab me if I was there, or whoever sat as his apprentice next to him, and have them "hold the mesa" until he returned after a violent bout of puking. He had in fact trained me to do this very thing and would often grab me with a gentle push toward the mesa when he stepped out. Not this time.

Without the shaman present, we sat and stood with the energy erupting and erupting as if this *white lightning* had no bottom or ceiling. I simply cannot find words for the feelings and state of perceptions we were experiencing. I stepped forward and took don Eduardo's rattle from the mesa and called everyone before me who had not been cleansed and one at a time performed the ritual cleansing. It had real impact as I worked directly on the energy lines. Many of us could see exactly what I was doing as we watched the sheets of energetic dandruff break loose and the vertical energy meridians brighten while the person experienced increased well-being, or visions or other positives. When Kamala came before me I'm not sure who blessed whom the most but touching her energy body was like stroking the ethers of heaven. Lorena came second to last and stroking her energy fields, striking the rattle along her meridians, was like igniting a volcano. My god, this woman, who was already so lit and energized, became supercharged with ecstatic outbursts and began to dance the power animals around the circle. The drumming, rattling and chanting spontaneously erupted again roaring throughout the mountain. The power animals filling Lorena and her movements were awesome and would soon become out of this world.

Big Beau came before me last and I cleansed him with the same respect and devotion given to all. What a powerful and unusual man! Every place on his energy body felt the same and equal to every other location. Immediately after I cleansed him he bowed to me, something totally voluntary and never mandatory. Even in that state of being I was touched, but I could tell he meant more than what was immediately apparent. It was a bow of respect, all right, but also the kind of bow one often gives before a martial contest. He left the circle to pick up an enormous branch and began raking the fire back and forth. Perhaps I left the circle to urinate, or perhaps I wandered briefly for a break from Beau's fire raking, but I recall looking toward don Eduardo's tent and distinctly seeing the silhouette of a woman inside with The Shaman. Without knowing how I knew who she was, at least what she was, and shuddered at some level realizing what Don Eduardo was facing. I felt an urgency to return to the circle immediately and did.

A long time went by and eventually we were all standing in circle watching Beau still raking the fire until he had spread out a deep lawn of reddish blue, orange and yellow coals stretching twenty feet long and ten wide. He had been traveling deeper and deeper into trance with his raking and eventually succeeded at standing everyone to attention, each of us witnessing him through outrageous states of perception and being. Just the physical accomplishment to get this fire to the coal state was a magnificent move on Big Beau's part and in those moments he was in charge. Moving everyone to a unified field of attention was a substantial move in this state and yet there he was doing it. We all directed our full attention toward Big Beau and frankly I doubt anyone knew what he was programming to do. I certainly didn't. Finally he threw down the branch, which resembled a lion tamer's bravado movement under the big top. The show had begun and all the lights dimmed while the spotlight shined on the center ring.

With athletic dexterity while remaining on his feet, he took off his shoes and socks and rolled up his pant legs. Everyone watched him in various states of ecstasy and profound altered consciousness. Big Beau stepped forward and stood before the coals, a warrior with presence emanating something truly fierce. Beau clasped his hands tightly together and pointed his two index fingers firmly straight down in front of his genitals while he arched his neck backwards. Looking up, he walked steadfastly across the glowing embers with purposefully long steps exactly how he would sometimes walk the trail, as if he were reaching and stepping onto a deliberate spot his radar had cleared. It was beyond impressive. It was galvanizing. It changed the mood entirely and a dark, though awesome, opportunity welled around us. Enormous respect and, yes, even love welled up in me with a strange energy that also disturbed me, all in an instant. Beau still had his back to us and had not yet turned around after walking across the coals. I bet many of us shared this ambiguous moment of extending gratitude while feeling extreme caution and not being clear just why. Big Beau turned around and faced us. He stood there, strong and powerful and blazing defiance.

Defiance? Why defiance? Many of us surely had the same disturbed reaction.

We were about to love Big Beau and instead of receiving it, he challenged us as though none deserved his respect, or we had flunked appreciation school for how powerful he was. His walk through the coals had been an act of power all right; I think everyone saw that and wanted to acknowledge his courage, his act, but he demanded we acknowledge something else. His superiority.

No question about it. He had truly done something magnificent. Yet it was propelled by something that was not peaceful so much as disturbing. We all felt it. His mood was intimidating, or trying to be, even though his act was profound at first, at least until he looked at us with a weird defiant energy in his otherworldly eyes. He was totally oblivious to the complete respect many of us felt for what he had just done *but he did not see that*. His stance really slammed the circle with encompassing complexity that was already off the chart. The shaman had left the circle. Or had he? Big Beau was displaying his power among us, totally galvanizing everyone's full attention, something extremely difficult to do and very much the hallmark of a shaman. The painful part, at least to me in the moment, was that we wanted to fully give that reflection to Beau. But who wanted to go where he did? Frankly, not a lot of us. I was becoming concerned and starting to feel internally challenged. When I took don Eduardo's rattle from the mesa, it was up to me to either "hold" the mesa, meaning the full attention and confidence of everyone present, or I must give it to another if I could not do that. Holding the mesa means holding the ceremony together with such internal coherence that no matter what happens, all are taken care of. I had initially intended to walk the coals until Beau turned around, making it impossible to affirm what he did. What was the move here? Should I answer Beau? Should anyone?

The Roshi stood up. What a magnificent figure he cut at the fire and there was no doubt he was a master. Was he about to walk the coals? My heart must have pounded as I anticipated one of the foremost Zen masters in the world about to display something beyond imagining. Then, completely unexpectedly, he turned his back to the circle and sat down with a dramatic flourish. He might as well have "mooned" Big Beau, such was his gesture. Without saying a word he gave his response to Beau. Then I "saw" why Beau did not respect our appreciation and perhaps why the Roshi turned his backside to him. Beau couldn't respond to us because he wasn't there. Beau, whoever Beau really was, had vacated entirely and this was an unadulterated force standing before us now in complete control. He had broken the shaman's ten percent rule and there was nothing left of Big Beau except his intentions without his charge over them. This was the dark general, the magic Kamala and Harmon had warned me about, and he meant to finalize his dominance. I felt a moment of compassion for Beau, wherever he was, because this tyrant occupying his corporeal space looked to me like a high price to pay to walk the coals. Then I shuddered looking at this daunting figure before us. I felt heavy for a moment, my rational mind trying to find somewhere inside to tell me what to do. There was no hope for that. I could not organize any coherent series of thoughts into normal thinking even if I had tried. All I could do was feel the intensity in the space and for a few moments it was crushing, presenting what I could neither accept nor control. Beau was challenging me to walk the coals but it was the "challenge" part that made it impossible to accept, yet if I didn't, then what?

My eyes spontaneously found Kamala's looking at me intently, and she communicated with a silent authority that fiercely grabbed me. "The feminine will answer, exactly as you requested," she emphatically communicated.

That I requested? my eyes asked. Kamala's non-verbal communication was so utterly lucid and clear that it forced me to notice that I had several layers of consciousness experiencing several levels of communication taking place at the same time. The part of me that for a while seemed concerned with what to do next was in fact an illusion, a vapid internal dialog that meant nothing, while another, deeper part of my being had been responding to Beau all along, and also to several others in the circle at the same time.

I *saw* her wordless communication with complete clarity and when I thought she was about to make her move, I felt an intense pressure to receive whatever Kamala was about to do. Something that I had requested? Immediately I wanted to bathe her with protective energy to sustain her intentions. Instead of moving, however, she rhythmically jutted her chin several times, pointing with her nose until she guided me to look over at Lorena across the circle. Lorena's energy was strong and radiant and her personhood was a joy-filled explosion about to occur. She was becoming more and more joyfully animated with breathtaking movements that moved our attention away from Big Beau and fully upon Lorena. Our drumming and chanting spontaneously started up again. The dark mood that had been creeping around us instantly vanished as Lorena's ecstasy lifted us all back into a celebration toward our higher purpose for being there.

Lorena was a powerful woman, who was in her early forties at that time, and it would be hard to say enough about her capacity for courageous abandon. Trained in off-Broadway dance and drama, she was a high-profile healer from New York. Knowing her a little, to me she was attractive exactly like a cabaret singer in the hottest nightclub in Berlin in the early 1930's: very unusual looks that normally would not attract much attention until you saw what she did. Movie stars can be like that: sometimes sultry, other times incredibly raw, often alluring to all the senses even though you thought her ordinary only a short while ago. One doesn't actually realize how physically strong a great cabaret performer is until ten drinks after the show is over and she's still raring to go. Lorena had stamina and energy with the best of us, and then some. After dancing in place as if something inside her was building a head of steam, almost in a single leap, like a leopard, she tore off her boots and socks and rapturously danced through the coals. She expanded everyone with love and admiration for her exquisitely feminine act of *power*. Her joy was such a contrast to the somber power Beau had shown us. The feminine did answer and then some. If anyone thought it was over, however, that feeling was short-lived.

As if in response, Big Beau stepped forward and stood before the coals once again. Still we held Lorena's energy and mood. Taking his palm-grip stance, index fingers pointed down in front of his genitals with his neck craning backwards, he repeated his dark and powerful walk through the coals except this time he turned around and slowly walked back through them. Part of it took my breath away and except for the defiant, competitive edge, it would have been utterly stupendous. Once again Big Beau stood there as if daring anyone to match him. It was impossible to know which aspect to be more stunned by: his dark warrior or his pathetic arrogance. There were many of us who could have walked the coals in a state of love but answering an intimidating challenge was another matter, and perhaps that was the dark general's real intention, to hawk it out of everyone with a threat to match his mood. To me it was ugly and intimidating but I also saw the exotic beauty in all of it. Still I asked The Spirit's guidance. What was called for?

Lorena began dancing wildly in place. For that matter so did everyone else at one time or another during this out-of-time drama, but none like Lorena. My, oh my, did The Great and Holy Spirit fill her that night. Her mind and life force was so connected with the higher realms that I doubt she had any choice about anything except to allow her body to be a vehicle expressing her deepest intentions. And she did. Dancing in place, her movements changed in patterns as she went farther and farther out, farther and farther in. With dazzling unconscious grace integrated in her movements, she divested all of her clothing, revealing something beyond profound that had nothing to do with her body's appearance. Her legs spread akimbo in a horse stance with her toes pointing outward, very much like Charlie Chaplin's famous walk except instead of a shuffle, she moved like a powerful gymnast. Her arms sometimes arched overhead like a ballerina, while her legs alternated a jumping rhythm that postured like Buddhist depictions of ancient goddesses. Her sheer joy and light-filled abandon could not have made it any clearer that what animated her was not what animated Beau.

Lorena's dance across the coals only set Beau off once again with increased intensity as he repeated his march through the coals while Lorena almost did leaps in place. Once again Beau turned and faced us from the edge of the coals and once again a complex well of emotion responded. Then something happened that even in our extreme states of consciousness I suspect shocked everyone. More than shocked, we were electrified. Even the Roshi was moved to turn back around and take on a sacred stance to watch.

Once again Lorena danced out into the coals with impossible movements, except this time she literally dived into the coals and shoulder-rolled across them, quickly landing on her feet again! My mind had already completely stopped. I had no dialogue in my head and I could only witness. WOW doesn't begin to capture that moment! It was like the phrase, "I could have exploded." Well, I did explode seeing that; I had a bursting feeling from the inside out. I saw Lorena's energy body wrapped with gossamer threads that threw her out like a yo-yo onto the coals and back up again. I could equally see her physical body go down into the coals like normal vision, and simultaneously her energy body riding on these energy tracers that were everywhere around us. One moment I might see an energy pattern appearing out of the coals in front of me the size of an apple pie and with enough distinctness and material substance that I could step onto it if I had wanted. Energy patterns would appear and disappear like fireflies, and for the few moments they were visible I felt as though I could reach and grab them if so inclined. They could be the size of a dot or something expanded into a ray or a pattern of energy, like a thick and solid brushstroke across the canvas. In those moments the touch would have been no different than touching the ground I stood on. Every time Lorena dived on the coals she landed on an apple-pie-size energy plop that supported her weight above the coals and something in her clearly knew to do this. If the pool of embers had been a lily pond, these were like the large lily pads bullfrogs and other nautical critters will use to walk the waters.

The first shoulder roll returned Lorena to her feet in that Charlie Chaplin shuffle-like stance and she continued her ecstatic movements. Spontaneously she did another shoulder role in the opposite direction and returned to the dancing position while still in the coals. Then she became wildly frenetic and started rolling and rolling and jumping up and down until suddenly an alarm went off in me. It felt like something had literally smacked me on the back of my head. A sober part of me realized that we were at a very dangerous moment. The medicine was cresting and we were all bursting, some with joy, some with an overwhelming intensity that was draining; some could no longer hold the energy and had fallen over. A few were becoming disoriented and afraid, likely uncertain which reality they dwelled in, and two people were vomiting at the edge of the circle. I still held don Eduardo's rattle and it was up to me to hold us together.

Lorena was continuing so wildly that it was not so simple to stop her. I did not dare to short-circuit her trance and potentially harm her on those coals, let alone assume the right to impinge on her energetic response to Big Beau. And whatever else she was doing. Nevertheless, her safety was my safety and all of our safety. I knew in my bones that the next few moments were my responsibility and that I had to act. Now. An enormous feeling welled up inside of me. I looked over and saw that even Big Beau was totally awed and stopped in his tracks by Lorena's ecstasy. He was standing there with his own dejected admiration as though he too was relieved that something bigger than his own ego had something important and beautiful to show him. Seeing Beau standing in the same reverent awe and respect for what was occurring in front of us was the clear and definitive signal that released me.

At that moment Lorena had just rolled to her feet, and I leaped into the coals and tackled her chest to chest with a fierce bear hug. My arms clamped instantly around her like a steel vice as I held her in the air without allowing her feet to touch the ground. Soot and charcoal poured into my nose and mouth and eyes from the black veneer covering her as she unconsciously thrashed in my grip, as if her body did not yet realize she was no longer on the ground, but I did not let go. As if on cue, a half dozen others jumped into the coals and grabbed her while we lifted her writhing and twisting over to the mesa where we sat her down. We firmly and gently held her until she came back around with enough awareness to let us put her clothes on. Then we continued our journeys. My sole intent was to remove Lorena from the coals for her safety without interrupting her continued journey. The medicine would keep us expanded until the sun rose, but it was no longer cresting and I could feel a steady state. For hours Lorena remained so full of grace and touched by *power* that just looking at her gave me a rush. The next morning she was entirely black with charcoal soot except for the whites of her eyes, and she did have two minor blisters.

The remainder of that night was among the most joyful reflections I have ever had. I called the formal ceremony to completion and declared our time open for the rest of the night. The medicine was no longer cresting and I had entered a stable, glowing condition of inner peace and wonder. My mind was so exceptionally clear that it allowed me to *see* into the nature of anything I thought about. It would be an enlightening several hours before sunrise with one last delightful encounter before I retired into my personal meditations. I fully realized that we had one final San Pedro ceremony the next evening for don Eduardo to complete the Marcawasi initiations, but for now I simply wanted to bask in the feelings that were overwhelming me. I felt loved, seen and known by a Creation that was everywhere and more than enough for me to rest in.

CHAPTER FOUR

Marcawasi Initiation after the Fire Ceremony

A couple of us held Lorena in our laps, no one had any kind of plan, it just happened naturally, though not normally. At first we all crowded around touching and holding her to stabilize her energy with ours. Someone spontaneously got up and came back with a boot, then someone else went and got a sock, and on it went, enacting a silent psychodrama except for the roaring within our inner experience that remained volcanic. What we looked at was still fluid and porous and multi-dimensional more than a stable solid. We knew she was safe when she cracked a joke about destroying her last clean pair of underwear. We were all getting sooty from touching Lorena and her unexpected verbalization humorously let us know she was OK without having to say anything further.

Not that she was any more coherently rational than the rest of us, let alone capable of carrying on a conversation. Her joke was another manifestation of *power* working through her. It was still very difficult, if not impossible, to talk because spoken words instantly sounded absurd or pathetic against the high frequency experience of our own perceptions. Talking was a kind of farting in the space and guaranteed to signal we were imbeciles, or it was simply impossible to speak whatever we meant to say because we kept losing the point by the second or third word. These were hours for action, for connection, for deep communication, for *seeing* and even falling apart and going out of our minds, but *not for conversation*. Everyone in this group was both experienced and disciplined enough not to go there, with a humorous few exceptions I will relate shortly. Eventually Lorena was on her feet and we all moved along to walk around the bowl, lie down, form small groups to meditate or to go off alone to continue our personal inner journeys.

The bowl had become dark, lit only by starlight and embers from the coals. At some level I was missing the lustrous firelight illuminating the walls as our stadium lighting. I turned toward the coals wanting to feel more energy and light. About that time several people went to the woodpile. Soon another fire burned brightly with red flames and no trace of blue. Once again the fire lit the bowl from end to end and it was very soothing. In stark contrast to the previous fire there were no looming shadows on the walls, and even more curiously there were hardly any shadows at all and none held a constant texture. I went and sat on a very comfortable rock outcropping along the rim facing the center, sitting about ten feet up from the bowl floor, and enjoyed hours of celestial meditations, visions, realizations and silence. At some point I realized that I had a view of everyone in the entire bowl more or less. Something like sitting on the fifty-yard line in a perfect seat with the best view. To my right I could see don Eduardo's tent on the little knoll with no sign of any activity within. Fifty yards to my left the fire burned brightly and people were variously moving around. In front of me, as though I was the audience watching a stage, everyone eventually walked past my gaze as though they were the cast in a play. Walking around the bowl, people would sometimes stop in front of me and salute, or bow, or throw a kiss, or laugh, or wave and some would not see me at all. If what I saw on the stage in front of me was any indication, I can only wonder what they saw in me sitting and watching them. It was sheer delight.

As I gazed out on the stage, the actors moved about and the play was constantly changing. The Caucasian Indian couple continuously walked around the bowl and passed me endless times, never once looking toward me, only straight ahead. As though they were in a trance, they walked and walked, around and around. They emitted a constant murmuring that I surely assumed was chanting or ritual praying of some kind, except whenever I *saw* them they seemed a little obsessed and not exactly peaceful. I didn't dwell on it since they pretty much looked that way to me most times anyway.

Eventually on one of their pass-bys, I realized they were talking to themselves and to each other. At first I think it tweaked my positive reaction and amazement. I thought I would surely hear holy utterances so I zeroed in on listening to them. It's not that talk never takes place during these super intense hours moving in and out of the *nagual*, but it had better be absolutely perfect, and brief, very brief, because that's all the words anyone can easily process. By this time I started to hear a few sentences from this couple, and I was expecting it to be some kind of miraculous dialogue. When I finally realized what I was hearing, it produced one of the most difficult moments of the entire evening because I wanted to burst out laughing to overcome being upset. I compassionately wanted to reach out to help them, while my warrior spirit was utterly disdainful of such outrageous indulgence. Yet another part of me *saw* it as absolutely perfect! These two were doing the same thing they had been doing the entire trip, critiquing and criticizing everything and everyone. Except now they had lapsed into a kind of trance about it and actually were unwittingly performing something shockingly powerful from a weird perspective, something that don Eduardo called dark sorcery, using ceremonial time to "bad mouth" your compadres. Their sentences were run-ons without stopping, first one then the other without pause or lapse or seemingly even to breathe. It was comical, it was sad, it was neither, however I wanted to see it. It was my choice entirely and not only was I aware of that, I sat there as if I were turning the channels and watching changing episodes of cosmic drama.

At one point I *saw* a longhaired hippie wearing bell-bottom jeans and a flower tie-dyed shirt walk to the center of the stage and stand there with his hands in his hip pockets the way teenage boys do. The Zen Roshi had not changed clothes, rather he was playing with ideas and memories and inviting me to participate, at least that is what I energetically perceived him to be doing. I was amazed, delighted and inspired all in one breath recognizing the Roshi's invitation to participate. No doubt whoever he saw in me inspired him as well, so I slid off my rock and ambled over to him with my own hands in my hip pockets, remembering what it felt like to be twenty-one talking with the guys. We had never talked about the part of his life that was frequently in the media, such as being a new age icon with political and social influence.

Sliding my hands knuckle deep in my hip pockets and letting my wrists drop limp I took my part in the play. "ZZ Top," I said.

"Hippie Blues in the Haight," he immediately replied with a friendly smile.

"Linda and Jerry," I said.

"You know that?" he asked with self-mocking surprise, or perhaps it was genuine.

"Don't forget Werner," I added purposefully, catching him further off- guard.

"You and Herb Caen," he winced and feigned being unprepared for my words while moving the word game a step ahead of me.

We both doubled over laughing, something we had done many times on this journey but never like this. Yes, I knew about Linda Ronstadt and then Governor Jerry Brown of California, who according to the tabloids sometimes were seen together around the San Francisco Zen Center, but I had never mentioned it. I knew he had a friendship with Werner Erhard, because I had spent a little time with Werner myself.

"Wrong there, Dick Tracy," he retorted. "Werner doesn't allow friends."

In spite of our previous joking I had always maintained a certain sense of decorum and frankly so did he. He was, after all, someone unique in the world. In these moments, however, he chose to stand there with me, just two guys keeping each other in stitches with biographical tidbits, except we transmitted ninety-five percent of the information in-between the words. It was haiku poetry more than linear conversation.

When the talking trance couple made a pass by, we could hear their criticizing us for disrespectful outbursts during sacred ceremony: ". . . and they walked on Father Fire with dirty feet and no respect and did not make offerings in proper sequence, and they failed to uphold the sacred pipe the way our chiefs would pray because they did not ask Mother Earth first. She was offended and besides, their ceremony is not holy because they did not ask permission of Father Sky to be on the mountain in the first place and their cactus juice is unclean because they whistle when they should kneel instead, and no one said their prayers. . ."

Theirs was a steady drone of one interpretation after another as though their minds had zoom-focused through a lens that filtered every detail from a bizarre perspective and set their tongues on automatic. When we heard their words, we started laughing so hard we almost passed out and literally fell over. It was uncontrollable mirth and we were gasping for breath and we still couldn't stop, it was that funny.

Our group was mostly composed of beautiful and spiritually disciplined people and while we were enjoying ourselves immensely, no one ever dropped a certain quality of spiritual sobriety. We were laughing with the invisible masters we had invoked to bless and safeguard our ceremonial time and they were laughing through us. The alternative would have been to react to the walking trance couple and potentially get hooked to whatever negative energy they might stir. Instead, we remained untouchable without ever directly engaging or judging them. The laughing shaman laughs to see the portions of reality that are simply too sad and difficult to approach any other way, as well as from sheer joyfulness for existence. All of us had been around these teachings about laughter's purpose and in these moments we lived them.

It's a well known phenomenon among aficionados of the San Pedro ceremony that somewhere toward the end of the journey a huge appetite begins to stir, sometimes with the same lustful intensity with which we had been devouring infinity for many hours. It's a powerful feeling, a fantastic "hungry hombre" kind of feeling. For some it's not until the next morning, for others the last hours before dark, but either way it's a huge appetite that indicates we were definitely ready and able to chow down. It's *necessary* since it's usually been fifteen hours, sometimes longer, since our last meal. When the right kind of food is available it's a phenomenal eating experience! It's a wise shaman who completes the San Pedro journeys with wonderful late night and morning meals. And that's how we always did it traveling with don Eduardo.

For instance, we might finish up at Machu Pichu late into the night and then walk all the way down the mountain to the train station, and then walk the tracks a few miles to Aguas Calientes, arriving anywhere between one and three in the morning. We would always have dinner at one particular café along the tracks that don Eduardo favored. I don't know how he did it since there were no phones. Our manner of travel made it impossible to tell this little one-room family café ahead of time to expect us, and cafés don't stay open that late when every other shop would be closed. This café was closed every time I was ever in Peru late at night without don Eduardo. The family that owned it always acted as though they were expecting don Eduardo to arrive any minute, no matter what hour we arrived. When don Eduardo arrived, they would immediately place a hot cup of coca de mate tea and a large bottle of beer in front of him. I never saw don Eduardo touch the tea. Very shortly a plate would arrive with fried eggs (easy up) and beefsteaks piled high with potatoes and vegetables. These ceremonies burn huge amounts of energy and even though the San Pedro itself is nutritionally fortifying, one of its many unique attributes, at some point the body simply has to be refueled. That certainly was not going to happen this night at Marcawasi, however, nor the next.

While laughing with the Roshi no one was thinking yet of food, though at some level we were all aware that nourishment was a critical factor the next two days. We were almost out of food except for Lifesavers and trail mix and maybe a few bananas. We had another day and night of work to accomplish before we could make the half-day walk to the village. It's a lot quicker to travel down than up. It was not even as simple as that because there were no restaurants in the village. No one had any illusions about starving, but it was a question of having enough energy for completing the final ceremony, or even having enough energy to remain warm in your tent, let alone walk down the mountain.

At the lagoon initiation don Eduardo declared there would be a final ceremony without a fire. Doing two San Pedro ceremonies in a row is demanding under the best of circumstances because it takes a great deal of internal psychic and physical stamina to insure a healthy and positive second experience. I think it was clear to all that don Eduardo meant to test us, and after all, we had all come for that purpose. Without substantial nourishment between the ceremonies, however, it became a critical choice that everyone had to face. Not participating in the final ceremony jeopardized if not canceled any initiation entitlement. That was never spoken, simply understood. But truthfully, after the fire ceremony I think there were only a handful who believed they would be initiated. Most wanted to participate in the final San Pedro ceremony, but everyone now had to seriously weigh the risk. It was really a question of how our bodies felt, *and our spirits*, and whether we had enough life force to take care of ourselves. No matter how urgently we may have wanted initiation by don Eduardo, if we could not hold ourselves together it wouldn't matter.

Somewhere in the back of all of our minds these kinds of realizations surely dwelled. Then I suddenly remembered a carefully guarded secret that I had told no one: a private and personal mission I intended to fulfill on this journey. The moment had come to make my move, the very moment I had planned for a long while. I would be taking care of myself in this precise kind of situation, except I had not counted on sharing with company. "Power cookies," I said.

The Roshi gave me a wide-eyed smile because we both knew that he had no idea what I was talking about, nor did anyone else. No one filled in a mental picture and we all knew it.

"Back soon," I said, creating an air of anticipation.

I walked across the bowl to my tent and retrieved a Quaker Oats cardboard cylinder that I had carried in my pack the entire trip, which was filled with homemade oatmeal cookies my eighty-five-year-old mother had made. They had been carefully sealed in my backpack the entire journey. I had saved them for this very evening, anticipating the late night munchies, although never anticipating the elevated importance they would serve in the group. Obviously, The Spirit foresaw this because the cookies were also something very serious between my mother and me. They were simple oatmeal cookies, with ingredients that had been perfected from an evolving family recipe, but the *intent* placed into them was meant to be life nourishing. I knew the importance of being in the mountains and needing fuel in-between meals. These cookies were an energized improvement over trail mix and a way for my mother to contribute and participate in what I was doing in Peru. She had been raised a Catholic and it took her a long while to understand, let alone accept, the path I had chosen and the cookies were her way of sending her blessing. My mother died six years later in the same moments I was enacting a San Pedro ceremony on a mountain top to escort her into the next dimension. I'll relate more about that in another book.

Our little group was incredulous, to say the least, when they finally understood what I was holding up in front of them.

"Power cookies," I said several times, holding up the oatmeal box.

"From your mother," one of the men repeated, as if he could not understand his own words.

Who knows for certain what any of them finally understood but the point got across when they put one in their mouths. This little experience for us was quite profound. Here we stood at the top of the world in the most exotic isolated wilderness for an exalted purpose, following a ceremony that was barely believable even while it was happening. We had not much food left, and out of nowhere arrived these cookies that tasted not only heavenly, they were truly *power cookies*. We felt their power go right into our energy bodies immediately. Foundational, fortifying with life force energy that immediately changed how we felt, and it stayed with us. It was as if we had eaten a substantial meal. I went around the bowl area and offered a cookie to as many as I could find before I finally went to my tent. I approached the trance couple with utmost respect and reverence, stated my case in two words, and they both accepted one. People were talking about it the next day, how nourished they felt from that cookie, while I was thinking about *power* and the unexpected if not outlandish ways it manifests. The feminine had arrived yet again.

I probably had slept for a couple of hours in my tent when I realized the sun was coming over the walls. A few clouds had come in and it was cooler light than on previous mornings. I felt like jumping up but I resisted because my normal morning urge to go and find a cup of hot tea was not going to happen this time. Eventually I got up after hearing others milling around, and I walked over to Lorena's tent just as she unzipped her tent and stepped out.

"This is just plain disgusting and it's all your fault," she said loudly, feigning being angry at me and trying not to smile as if it physically hurt to do so.

I could only see the whites of her eyes while every other part of her was coal black. I tried not to laugh but a few snickers slipped out. She peeled off her jeans inside out and shook them vigorously while telling me she would never forgive me, and she pledged that she would get even. The feelings underneath her words, however, were a strained combination of gratitude and concern with a strong dose of mirth. I warmly accepted her comments for the feelings of kinship they conveyed. I could tell that she was just beginning to consider what had happened and for that matter so was I. She had never before been on coals and had no conscious thoughts about it before the ceremony, nor had I. I gave her a hug and walked on, not wanting to say much at that point either. We had a final ceremony ahead of us and regardless of what had happened the night before, it was necessary to turn our sights forward. I grabbed a small, black speckled banana before I walked out of the bowl to amble around the high country.

Ancient Stone Ghosts

Once out of the bowl all I could see was a rolling stone floor that extended for miles. This expanse, except for the hint of the receding mountaintop, could not be seen from below. I was probably strolling for an hour and a couple of miles from the bowl when I came upon an ancient cemetery similar to the ones I had seen in the Nazca desert. Coffins made of stones and about chest high were sitting on the rolling granite floor, which had made it impossible to bury anything. All of them, maybe a hundred, had been broken into. Stealing the remains of ancient graves was a lucrative business in Peru. At this altitude I doubt the grave robbers found much more than rot and decay, although ancient jewelry could have been preserved. I kept my distance and did not try to inspect them. It just wasn't my interest, but it was fascinating to find something so unexpected.

One night when he had awakened me from sleep, don Eduardo told me that the only one at risk is the person who actually breaks into a grave. A grave robber, who looked like an inner city wino, had appeared at our motel late one night in Nazca and wanted to sell us his wares. I'll never forget the odor from the plastic garbage bag he carried. When he untied it I thought I was going to puke. Not only did don Eduardo appear to have zero olfactory response, he patiently pawed through every weaving and ceramic and piece of jewelry, pulling items from that bag and laying them on his bed before us. Remember not to judge, I thought, but I had to excuse myself for air a couple of times. I was grateful it was don Eduardo's room and not mine. That smell had been as close as I ever wanted to get to the graves they came from. Looking out over this extremely ancient burial ground, I wondered how long it had been since anyone had lived on top of this mountain. I would find out later that no one actually knew and it was a place that had hardly been researched, if at all. I took some tobacco from my hip pack and spent a few minutes making an offering to the spirit(s) of this place before I walked on.

Soon I came to an exceptionally flat area many miles in diameter. Slightly rolling smooth granite, like an enormous pavement, spread in all directions, which made for leisurely walking. The extended landscape was dotted with enormous boulders that each stood alone, perhaps a half dozen or more were spread widely apart. At first I barely noticed them spread among the vast expanse and when I did they looked "naturally" unusual, like natural earth formations always do. These boulders turned out to be the size of small and large houses when I eventually walked near one. I noticed it was hard to tell in the distance the size of the boulder and the perspective easily got lost. They could look huge or ordinary in the distance. These large, rough and uneven rocks were full of indentations and crevices and looked like they had been set down out of nowhere on this unlikely flat surface, but they were unexceptional otherwise. I walked on not thinking any more about it.

I was deep into my thoughts, enjoying my stroll and thinking about last night's ceremony when I was so completely caught off-guard by an overwhelming image that I reflexively reeled around while spontaneously and desperately reaching in my pants pocket for my pocketknife to defend my life. I must have slipped on pebbles and fallen down in the process, because the adrenaline was pumping so hard in my temples that it sounded like drums going off. I felt these could be my final moments on this earth. I tend to have exceptional peripheral vision but that may not have had anything to do with it. I was suddenly, in a split second, aware that "a giant lizard" was over my shoulder and since it was huge and real, I reacted as though it was about to eat me. This overwhelming threat, which my rational mind could not process, produced one of those heart-stopping kinds of moments. What I perceived was so completely outlandish that it froze my hard drive and I only had raw animal reactions left. I was down on one leg hoarsely panting as though a dinosaur was poised to bite my head off. Looking up, I was veritably dazed for a moment, utterly confused.

Where was it? Had I seen it? There's nothing there! My thoughts raced and that da-da-da-da Twilight Zone music played in the background. *But then it was there again*, huge, and almost on top of me! But where was it? The intense silence and my aloneness amidst this vastness made me feel vulnerable and secure at the same time, while my head jerked this way and that way until I was satisfied that nothing was nearby. Slowly, cautiously, now holding my knife, I stood up and carefully looked around me. Then I saw it again and for a moment my heart skipped. In front of me stood a gigantic reptile, crouching on this enormous stone floor as a perfect, and I mean perfect, portrait. It was all there right down to the detail of his lizard eyes: the angular bumpy nose and face, the tuck of his enormous legs receding into his hips; he looked as if he were about to race the distance between us and with a zip of his tongue snap me up like a fly.

I was momentarily stunned and then slowly charmed and decidedly dumbfounded. My mind could barely accept what was looking back at me and yet there it was. This boulder, this edgy and formless rock, once I had walked into a certain angle of view a couple of hundred yards away, suddenly looked exactly like a giant lizard and something very much alive. One moment it was simply a rock I was looking at directly or peripherally. After a few steps, I was now looking at something that looked back at me with such crystal clear appearance, form and shape that my mind stopped. It did not look like a stone carving, not at all. I could see that it was made of rock, and yet it looked alive, at least more alive than anything I had ever imagined carved in stone. Not only that, looking at it produced a strange perceptual blur, a little like chiaroscuro in art technique, with an effect that made size and space and proportion and distance more a matter of what I thought I saw as much as what was there. It was even more complex and unnerving than that. When I stood up and partially looked away for a moment, the lizard then appeared to move from being far away to closing in on me, my peripheral vision causing it to appear closer and more enormous and once again affecting my senses as though I was being chased down by a monster. Directly looking at it made it appear smaller and farther away and when I moved my eyes it could appear to move in my peripheral vision until it was next to me.

What am I looking at? I asked myself. It took me more than a few moments for my mind to rationally decide on an interpretation.

There's a place in Santa Cruz, California, called the "Mystery Spot," where walking into a certain room the perspective becomes utterly bizarre, making it appear that far is near, and up is down. That's what was going on here, and then some. I walked ahead for maybe a hundred yards and this reptile remained in perfect view and then within a few yards it would disappear and all I would be seeing was a gigantic rock. Getting a little excited about this amazing discovery, I walked around in a lot of directions checking out the view of the rock lizard until I had a thought. I started looking around in the distance. There were more than a few of these "rocks" spread around me. I looked at another one. Oh my god, I thought, I can't believe it! Seventy degrees to my right, maybe a mile or so away, sat an enormous rabbit, complete with sticking-up ears, nose and whiskers, sitting on its haunches like the lizard and twice the size. I became more overwhelmed with these stones than the kids back at camp watching the women. I wandered around in every direction almost in a daze, sometimes tripping from not wanting to take my eyes off these incredible creations that would change and almost appear to move depending on my perspective. I walked and walked and finally got another rock to reveal its secret, an animal of some kind that I did not

113

recognize. It looked like some kind of gopher to me, or an entity of some kind.

Eventually I headed over to the rabbit and when I got within fifty yards of it, the form disappeared. For a long time I walked around that boulder, the size of a large house, trying to ascertain every location it was visible and when it would disappear. When I walked up to the rock it looked like nothing except a big rock. It had no, and I mean zero, marks on it that remotely indicated it had been chiseled, carved or in any way touched by a human hand. It looked jagged in a lot of places, and I realized the shadows affected its appearance as much as the shape of the stone, which otherwise appeared entirely natural. I wondered if there were certain times of the day that the forms took shape and was hesitantly curious what they might appear like in moonlight. The more I realized the utter fantastic accomplishment of what I was looking at, the stranger and stranger it became. Not only had I never seen anything like it, I had never known that any such thing existed. Who would make such a thing, and why?

I was only able to personally confirm three of these strange boulders to contain hidden structures, but I assumed they all did. To check them all out would have taken a considerable amount of walking and taken more than a day or two. I was heading out to check on another boulder in the distance when I heard some excited yelling coming from a mile or more in the direction of the bowl. I turned around to head that way and to tell my companions about what I had discovered. I pinpointed that the yelling was coming from the rugged cliff faces behind our bowl, so I followed the sounds. Soon I was standing in front of a cliff face about a quarter mile high and perhaps a hundred or more yards wide. I could see there were several from our group trying to climb the cliff face and they were yelling excitedly to each other.

When they saw me coming, they started yelling even more. "Do you see it," came the chorus. "Do you see it?"

At first I thought someone had lost something important and they were trying to enlist my support. Great, I thought, we're only spread out over a mountain face a half-mile wide and someone lost his or her flashlight. I didn't feel like spending my time looking for lost articles and was not sure how to get their attention to tell them of my recent and amazing discovery. I walked around a rocky bend trying to see if there was a path leading to my companions on this ledge, who were now excitedly yelling at me with more intensity. Someone must have lost something important for all that noise, I thought and then I saw it! I couldn't take my eyes away as surely my jaw dropped. That entire cliff edifice contained a face with utterly clear and detailed features looking as though the eyes responded to seeing me. It wasn't only that the eyes could see me; it was that kind of look that made me feel the eyes were "consciously" focusing on me.

"We can't see it this close," one of the men hollered at me. "Do you see the face from where you're standing?"

I saw it all right, and one more time on this walk I was speechless. Several times I walked back and forth along the bottom of that cliff face while the entire face, and most especially the eyes, *followed me as I walked.* I thought that was a craft that belonged to twentieth century photography and Renaissance art. Yet here was this stone cliff with an entire face that continued to stare directly at me within perhaps a forty-five-degree range of angle, maybe more. It was definitely a male face, with hair down the sides of the head, impossible (for me at least) to give it any racial characteristics. The face was long and not short; the stare was neither friendly nor unfriendly, also forceful and strong and unabashedly looking right into me. Just like the giant animal rocks, the cliff face upon inspection looked only natural with not the slightest trace of anything artificial having touched it. Whoever did this, I thought to myself, was likely the guy I'm looking at, or someone very important to whoever created the face. But how? Why? Who were these people? Who *are* these people was my next thought.

I had a creepy feeling go up my neck. I did not want to be looking at this face any longer, or more precisely I did not want it to be looking at me. The wonder and intrigue quickly evaporated for no overt reason except suddenly I felt cautious. Something in me started to look at all this quite differently. I stopped being on a stroll and brought myself back into mental alignment with what I was there for. This is Marcawasi, where sorcerers have been initiated for centuries, and while I did not know what I was looking at, it was clear that I needed to return to my tent and rest up for the evening's ceremony. All of these otherworldly stone edifices were suddenly too entertaining, too attractive, too inviting and it no longer felt energizing. Then I realized it. This face was trying to draw energy from me. Nothing external happened, it was just a feeling. But a very clear feeling and I could *see* the face doing it. That was eerie. It wanted to be so utterly compelling that I would let it into my feelings and when I did I noticed a drain. It was like getting sunburn, it felt great at first but by the time you noticed the burn it would be too late. Whoever constructed all this had a mighty purpose that was more than entertainment. This was not art we were looking at. I did not like the feeling of entertainment it was producing in my companions. I gave an encouraging yell to return to camp but they stayed out there for quite a while. I carefully noted with some relief on my walk back to camp that even though this cliff face loomed high over the bowl, it was also far enough back on the mountain that the face could not see our ceremonial space.

Clouds had been creeping in all afternoon and the temperature had been steadily dropping. The energy in the camp was low and that concerned me. I climbed into my sleeping bag in my little one-person tent and drifted for a couple of hours, not really wanting to think about those stone edifices above us. I awoke from a semi-sleep knowing it was soon time for the final ceremony. I checked my energy and overall condition internally and had to be honest with myself: it was eighty percent at best. I was not hungry, for which I was very thankful, but a part of me would have preferred to head for dinner instead of ceremony. I stepped outside my tent to urinate and sternly cleared that thinking from my consciousness. It worked. I reentered that cherished feeling of being privileged to be there at all. Listening to the sounds of the camp waking up from most everyone napping brought it all back: the joy, the wonder, the exquisite tension that I intended to embrace as best I could. Whatever inner resources I had left, I told myself, would be enough. There would be the rest of my life for good meals. Tonight would never come again, so let me drink deeply from this well and accept all that is offered.

I noticed the temperature had dropped again. I had thermal underwear and my clothing was substantial so I was not too concerned. I did start to think about my fellow travelers, however, and wanted to know how they were doing. There was some time before we needed to gather so I went over to a group of tents specifically to check on people. Two people from different directions immediately approached me, both concerned about tent mates who were sick. I visited a tent where a doctor in our group was checking on a man who was sweating profusely. Only a few hours ago he had been happily climbing all over that cliff face and now he didn't look very well. He took my hand and apologized for not having the physical reserves to attend the ceremony; he meant no disrespect to anyone but he just could not make it. I assured him that staying in his sleeping bag was the right choice, and I did not mirror any concern though I had plenty. Having gone through profuse sweating a couple of times, I knew it could be very dangerous when the temperature is very cold. Your clothing along with the sleeping bag gets drenched from sweat and later you start to freeze. I told him to change his shirt during the night and went over to the next tent.

Not one but two women were huddled, and it was obvious as soon as I looked at them that they were not sick but exhausted and very low on energy. They had also climbed all over that cliff face but I did not say anything about it except to ask if they had brought anything back from their walk. One of them had and I threw it as far away as I could. We had a focused conversation while others gathered around and several more people decided they would not attend the final ceremony for the same reason. Their fuel was spent. They no longer desired to be initiated. There was no complaint or self-pity or feeling of failure. It was simply a matter of seeing the truth and not requiring any judgments toward self or others. It also made me feel better about the situation because a number of people low on energy but ambulatory could look after each other. We set it up that way, changing a few tent residences, identifying who had any trail mix left and so forth, and I was able to let it go until morning. I walked away, turning my full attention to the ceremony, knowing everyone was taken care of, at least the best we could manage under the circumstances.

The Final Ceremony

I anticipated the clarion call from Beau's horn, or whatever he used to make that sound, but it never came. The clouds had come in blanketing the sky; there was zero starlight and flashlights were mandatory to find our way. I saw a trail of lights starting to head in a single direction and I knew don Eduardo had emerged from his tent. We went to a corner of the bowl where ebbing hills gradually inclined around us before turning into the high walls. Until we were there I had not noticed there was a little alcove perfectly suited for sitting in ceremonial circle. Don Eduardo did what he often did before a ceremony and I did the same. We found the biggest rock we could carry and brought it over for a seat. I was frankly surprised that only a few others did the same. Nothing wrong with sitting on the ground, I had done it countless times, but as the hours go by, being off the ground makes a huge difference when it's cold out. Little did I realize it would make minimal difference this night. The North was about to set in with a cold challenge.

Instead of sitting next to don Eduardo, I sat at nine o'clock to his left. I did that spontaneously without thinking about it. I recall no one that night sat directly to his right in a ceremonial apprentice position. I did not think about it until I was sitting down and then let it go. If he wanted me to his right he would have called me over. The mood, timing and tempo of this ceremony are entirely different than the fire ceremony. First and most obvious there's no fire. It can be ecstatically exquisite to adjust your eyes to see, with the aid of San Pedro, all of the wondrous light and life that resides in the dark. Most ceremonies are conducted that way. This was the first time I had sat down to a ceremony and did not like the dark. Specifically, it was cold, not only the temperature but also the darkness itself. I knew the difference because I had done ceremony in another desert below freezing and the darkness was utterly welcoming. This darkness was somber, heavy, cold and weighty, not at all the feeling I welcomed to embrace. It was obvious this ceremony was going to be demanding and nothing like last night.

Don Eduardo commenced the ceremony in a predictable manner. The circle was sitting instead of standing as we were during most of the fire ceremony. Except for our trip before his mesa to drink the San Pedro, don Eduardo was the only person externalizing with his chants and singing and rattling. Everyone else was on a personal and silent inward journey transported by his sounds and the profound effects of his medicine. Not so typical of his ceremonies, however, were his long periods of silence in-between his sounds. During the San Pedro intoxication, one could very easily not notice his silence or virtually anything external to your own inner world although sometimes silence can become so loud it's as if the entire universe is a single loudspeaker between your ears. But I certainly noticed don Eduardo's long pauses. I was focused, deeply internal amidst a vast inner landscape surrounding me, and simultaneously right there on my rock in the circle; my eyes were wide open even when they were closed, watching don Eduardo's every move, or so I believed.

No one had a clue what exactly finalized initiation in don Eduardo's world, and he had said nary a word about it that I knew of. We had signed up for the initiation journey to Marcawasi but knew very few details after that. Was it finally a moment when he stood up and gave the initiate a ribbon, handed over his rattle, or what? It was his blessing that we all sought, however, and I'm certain no one, including myself, cared very much about the form in which it was delivered. What few of us realized is how much of that possibility depended upon matters beyond what don Eduardo could govern. It was becoming increasingly clear as I sat on that rock deep in the San Pedro trance that don Eduardo wanted to give every drop of his shamanism to all of us if we could only hold and receive it. I admired him for that and believed I understood. After all, what could possibly honor him more than to receive what he had received from those gone before in order to continue the *knowledge*? Don Eduardo did not especially think in terms of lineage so much as a responsibility to pass forward what had been given to him. It was *knowledge* that got passed and up to the individual what to do with it.

What seemed like hours and hours later, still no one knew what consummated the act of deliverance for don Eduardo. We had been sitting and sitting with don Eduardo rattling and singing, interspersed by long silence, and then rattling and whistling and singing and taking another long silence. This had been repeating for a long enough time that we were on the downward side of our San Pedro journey, so it was probably six or more hours later, maybe even eight. Ordinary reality was beginning to intersect our awareness, becoming so conscious that I knew I was sitting on a rock in the dead of night with no fire and it was blitzkrieg cold out. I mean the kind of cold that seeps down into your bones and begins to affect you at core levels. Before the cold began to intrude into my consciousness, I believed I had stayed vigilant to the ceremonial space while participating in a deep inner world. The cold finally drove me into complete external awareness, although far from ordinary consciousness to be sure. For the very first time in a ceremony, ever, I became aware of my butt and how freezing it had become and questioning my purpose for being there.

About that time a woman stood up with a blanket wrapped around her. I could tell she was shivering and she left the circle to return to her tent. That was the first time I noticed there were several others missing from the circle. That shocked me for a moment, realizing that I had had major lapses in my attention when I thought I had none. I had not been aware of anyone leaving the circle, which is entirely understandable given the depth of the inner world I had entered, but I thought I had retained a level awareness for everyone in the circle. Obviously I had not. I would roughly guess there were twelve people remaining out of an initial eighteen or so. Don Eduardo did a particular series of chants and whistles followed by "insurance" whooshes when anyone left the circle and still I had failed to notice many.

He continued his rattling and singing for quite awhile until the next silence. Was this what he had been waiting for? Who would be left in the hard core group sitting through the cold? I didn't like it but had enough internal discipline to interrupt that thinking as soon as I realized it. I had come too far to start judging don Eduardo's shamanism. That was a timely mental correction for me, because just then don Eduardo did the incomprehensible. I couldn't believe my eyes! I was incredulous when he held up the seashell of nose juice and called me to the mesa.

I was also physically revolted and my mind started to react. He was serving nose juice at this late hour? Drinking that stuff when you're still cresting with San Pedro in an ecstatic state is one thing. Drinking it during the downside of the journey in butt-freezing cold on the second night of ceremonial work was something else.

I halted the dialogue going off in my mind and brought my entire mind to complete silence. Utter stop and I locked the safe door. In one moment his hand above the mesa holding that shell looked like a lot of unpleasant interpretations in my head. In the next moment it looked like nothing other than a hand above the mesa with a shell that belonged to me. I stood up and walked the circle to the mesa and took the shell, drinking it nose down without much hesitation. He handed me two more shells that I nosed down and then he told me to turn around. Immediately, I saw a peculiar whitish fog about fifteen feet high and wide sliding down the hillside until it hovered behind the circle.

I believed don Eduardo meant for me to *see* it, but wondered if it was simply a fog phenomenon. I had been in every kind of fog for protracted periods. Like fractals, there is an explicit predominance in the chaos. This was not fog. I saw it creeping along the ground sliding its tendrils forward onto the rocks and moving its mass forward with a sense of purposefulness. As it moved, it maintained a coherence of form and never drifted into elongating wisps like fog always does. I could not see through it even though it gave the impression of being very faint. I watched a boulder disappear as it moved in front of it. It was ten feet behind the circle, facing me directly from the opposite end while I stood in front of the mesa. It looked more like a cloud of light, except the light was evenly dispersed with no central point, making it appear like some kind of meta substance that was neither pure light nor pure cloud but something in-between. It was faint though utterly distinct from everything darker around it and had a strange luster that evoked both intense attraction and sober caution, such as standing in front of a bear or a mountain lion in a primitive environment. I have stood eye to eye with both animals at arm's length in the wild and the feeling was similar: awed by the danger and riveted by the beauty of the moment when it's too late for a pinch test, or even to breathe and impossible to blink. I had an overwhelming feeling "it" was entirely conscious, aware, and deliberately moving toward us.

Then it rapidly lurched forward and hovered over the shoulders of a man in the circle. If he had stood up, the foggy form would have been almost twice his height. Besides don Eduardo and myself, only a few others gave any indication of seeing what had suddenly become the main attraction. Perceptually and experientially this movement was momentous even though I did not know what I was seeing. I stood there empty, completely receiving what I was witnessing on all channels but allowing no mental playback at that time. Don Eduardo erupted when it hovered over the Roshi. A long series of chants followed with two words constantly interspersed, the Roshi's personal first name and the word "shaman." I was transfixed *seeing* this, recognizing that something important was happening for the Roshi and almost disturbed that only Lorena, Kamala, Beau and a few others gave any indication of watching. Eventually the Roshi twisted around while remaining seated and looked up at this hovering light cloud with a stern gesture of indifference. Not disrespect, not rejection, no personal reaction, simply indifference. He then turned around and resumed his meditation posture and this cloud quickly moved back up the hill and disappeared. I walked back around to my rock and sat down and drifted off into I'm not sure where. Don Eduardo had stopped singing and the silence pulled me into my own inner world, assisted by scrunching up for warmth and burying my face in my lap.

Wearing a wool cap and a jacket hood with layers of clothing, I sunk down into my inner world as far as I could find to go. However long I was there was too short. Bursting into my inner world I felt a cold blob in my stomach as if something tangible had pushed in through my lower back and soured there. Suddenly my stomach heaved and yanked me out of my inner reverie and I discovered that my face was still buried in my lap. I was shivering intensely when a second burp oozed the taste of the nose juice into my throat until I was gargling it. The urgency to puke exploded unrestrained. In spite of the cold, I sprang to my feet like a wild animal lifting off, simultaneously whirling around to expel the nose juice with a seamless move that I had perfected from necessity over the years. I landed on all fours and I roared like the jaguar, intentionally dominating the experience while totally submitting, as one must. There's no way around it with Peruvian shamanism. I could hear don Eduardo blasting off at the mesa, chanting my name, alternating the word "shaman" as he had done with the Roshi, while I roared the last drops from my guts.

Somewhere between wiping my mouth and lifting my head I was stunned to realize that I was kneeling on all fours entirely *within the light cloud*. I don't recall if I could perceive the ground but all I could see was a whitish fog like meta substance that was faintly luminous with evenly dispersed light throughout. It was all around me and I could not see anything outside it. My mind was still in the silence and I didn't react, except I had the exact feeling that I was nose to nose with a powerful wild animal. Without any vestige of fear or attraction, simply aware, I pushed myself up onto my feet and turned back around and ended up kicking my rock and then grabbing it to hold myself up. Before I could have any thoughts about it, the fog moved back like an animal backing away from an interest not entirely wanting to leave. I felt its extreme cold receding.

I watched the light cloud move away in the distance behind don Eduardo. I was physically, mentally and emotionally ready for the ceremony to be done and was now verging on exhaustion. My thoughts and feelings were rapidly becoming too normal. All I wanted to do was go lie down and get warm and close my eyes. Don Eduardo continued rattling and singing and rattling and singing and rattling and singing. It made no sense to me. A few more people got up and left and don Eduardo was still rattling and singing. I was shivering so violently and becoming so uncomfortable that it drove me virtually out of the journey space entirely. I looked over at don Eduardo.

Driven by the cold, or a deeper hidden perception, or both, for the first time I was done with ceremony and none of it looked appealing. A judgment came to the surface of my mind, one of a handful I had been fighting since day one. This looked more like surviving an ordeal than a spiritual initiation. There were six or eight left and by now everyone was simply hanging on from sheer discipline but the joy was gone. The meaning, the purpose, the ecstasy had disappeared although I was entirely awed at the physical capacity of don Eduardo to still be rattling. He was not nourishing me, however, and I don't think anyone else. I admired it but I didn't like it and I didn't like feeling that way. The freezing in my blood vessels made it impossible to feel otherwise. There was no ceremonial mood left in me and the ecstasy was over. Why wasn't the ceremony over?

At a certain point shivering adds to your warmth but that can only go on for so long. Throwing up in that cloud had removed any vestige of warmth I retained. I tried many times to signal don Eduardo internally but I could not contact him. I had reached a crisis once before and was all too familiar with the dangers of hypothermia. It was weighing on my mind that I had made a pledge to loved ones back home to stop short of certain injury if I knew it to be imminent. I was within minutes of losing any control over my body. Finally I stood up, stamped my foot hard by the sound of it, although I could not feel it. I bowed and walked out of the circle to find my way to a very cold tent and sleeping bag. The thermometer on my tent zipper said ten degrees Fahrenheit. Just as I was zipping up, I heard people coming in and knew the ceremony had completed. I offered a deep heartfelt salute to Beau and Lorena and the Roshi and those who stayed to the last. I shivered in a curdled ball in my sleeping bag, all too aware of the nylon pad between the freezing ground and me. I guess I didn't have it in me after all, was my final thought. A few more minutes and it would have been done. Could I have gone another few minutes, or was it my departure that brought the ceremony to a stop? I think I started to crucify myself with second-guessing and self-judgment but fortunately I was too cold for much of that. Eventually I warmed enough to drift off.

There was no sun coming through the clouds on a cold and dreary morning that came very quickly. My first thought coming into consciousness was gratitude that I felt warm. I had gotten into my sleeping bag with all the clothes I had worn the night before, many layers over thermals. My little thermometer now read 27 degrees. Things were looking up, I thought. I lay there as long as I could until the urge to pee finally got me out of my tent. Boy, the air was crisp. I looked at the oatmeal box and remembered I had already licked the crumbs. People were moving around the bowl and it was obvious the next move was to walk down the mountain as soon as don Eduardo said OK.

I was in a strange mood as I reflected upon last night's ceremony, which had ended only a few hours earlier. I had not remained at the circle until don Eduardo finished rattling and what fact could be plainer. I didn't measure up. Don Eduardo's initiation turned out to be some kind of ordeal to the last man, and I wasn't one of them after all. I could not get upset about it and yet I cared and felt disappointed in myself. But I think I even felt a little relieved. Standing in the freezing air looking across the bowl at that ridiculous orange tent surrounded by a colorful herd of baby tents, I knew *it had all been worth it*. Totally, every moment, right down to the soreness I felt throughout my body. I felt deep gratitude once again for everyone in that bowl and for everything that had occurred during the entire journey.

Did I really believe, I began to wonder, that anyone could be a "shaman" in our world? Our society and our culture have no such lock to fit that key; it simply doesn't exist in the Western world. Even in Peru I daresay that much of the European heritage population would feel the same. Or so I was arguing to myself and to this day I know that to be true. Shamans as they have existed since our origins do not have a place in modern society unless they are changed so much as to bear little resemblance to their origins. Still I was disappointed and I was pretty upset with myself. Even if I had passed don Eduardo's initiation I had never planned to advertise it. I had a perfectly viable identity in California and did not need to call myself a shaman. But the fact that I could not acknowledge something to myself loomed like a great loss in my psyche. Now that the spirits of this place and everyone else knew I had left the ceremony, I felt released from an impossible pursuit that had not left me alone my entire life. Shamans had crossed my path since childhood but now it was done. There was nothing further to pursue, so I accepted it, or so I told myself. I told myself it didn't matter even though I had slept and dreamt this path for years. Of course it did. Big time! The fact staring me in the face that I had not accomplished something important to me was difficult to accept.

Looking across the bowl at the tents and at people slowly moving around shifted my attention to where it belonged. I became very concerned about getting us all down the mountain safely. Suppose it started to snow or rain, or the temperature dropped further? Was everyone OK? Walking across the bowl I realized that I was feeling lots of different emotions and attitudes. Some of these magnificent people held their ground and they did not walk off until don Eduardo was done. How do I look them in the eye? I must have had tunnel vision with my thoughts because I barely noticed don Eduardo bounding out of his tent until he was walking right next to me.

"Randy," he said, warmly putting his arm around my shoulders. "Not many shamans have ever done that one, Amigo! You caught her off-guard and made her wait. If I had not seen it with my own eyes I would not believe it possible. You placed your face in her lap and she couldn't move until you were done licking her. She liked it so much you made her wait. *Power* moved you in a way only a shaman could do."

At first I had no idea what he was talking about. I was simply feeling relieved, even joyful that don Eduardo was feeling so warmly toward me. He obviously wasn't disappointed in my failure and that meant a lot to me. I still wasn't getting his meaning, however, only enjoying his warmth.

"You grabbed her so fast she couldn't move," he said as if amazed. "And with your tongue in her pussy, no less" he added with gestures of comically serious disbelief. "You turned the tables on her. She thought she was there to grab you!"

I still could not organize my thoughts coherently enough to appreciate what don Eduardo was trying to get across to me. Who did I grab last night? Oh no, did I grab one of the women? Is that why people had left the circle and I had not noticed? Oh no, did I lose it? What is he telling me? Did I finally come all this way only

127

to have disgraced myself in the end? Then, slowly his meaning started to sink in. He postured like a jaguar in a powerful squatting stance, letting out an outrageous roar that clearly resembled a person puking while jutting his tongue like he was licking something obscene. Then something peculiar like a sensation in the back of my head visibly shook lose and I then understood what he was saying as a realization flooded into my total feelings, mind and body. He was talking about that light cloud, that strange white fog that was some kind of "her" in his shamanism. In jumping through the air like a jaguar leaping I had landed on "her" and in the act of puking she was compelled to wait until I was done. Except, how is that possible or even real?

I was simply amazed at this man's worldview. I stood there transfixed staring at don Eduardo almost star struck by his certainty. One more time I was deeply affected by how he perceived reality and the effect it had on me. He instantly shifted my perception of what had happened the previous night and caused me to become aware of another level of experience that fit exactly with what he was pantomiming and telling me.

Whether I would have ever reached this level of awareness without don Eduardo's instruction I will never know, but suddenly I was remembering it vividly. While I sat huddled on that rock with my face buried in my lap, several times during the ceremony I felt this intense cold "approach," a cold whose intensity was penetrating my energy body. And it did have a feminine allure and my mind responded (if in fact it was "my" mind?) sometimes with vividly erotic visions so real they would absorb me totally. I was deeply buried in those visions and only now realizing how I had been unaware of parts of the outer ceremony. After several passes when she came down from the hillside and leaned behind me, the very last time "she" approached late in the ceremony, after the nose juice, the feeling in my gut became more upsetting than the iceberg feeling on my butt. It was a methane ice feeling expanding into my throat as well as the nose juice that I whirled around to expel but at the same time a deep and real part of me was responding. I meant to throw it out and did so. Insofar as intending to make "her" wait for me in the process, let alone engage in some kind of unnatural sex act with a semi-material being, inferentially a sorcerer who once inhabited a female body, well, I could just stand there and marvel to understand don Eduardo's meaning. It was beyond humbling. I had not been consciously aware of that light cloud approaching me, let alone intending to puke on "her" but I now realized something in me clearly and consciously interacted with her. I felt "her" presence and her penetration even though I was buried in my own lap, and I was enjoying her attention up to that final heave, but not until then did I *think about it* that way. *At the time I simply acted.*

"Last night I thought you would never be done with her," don Eduardo added. "You kept us out late. Only a few could wait for you but it was amazing to watch. Thank you, my friend. It was worth it. Now you understand enough of the shaman that it will never leave you alone."

I didn't see it coming. Don Eduardo had presented a level of understanding completely opposite to my own judgments, at least the thought I had woken up with. I had fallen into some kind of mental ego loop during part of the ceremony (delusional from cold?) and thought don Eduardo was doing it to me by droning on until I had to leave the ceremony. Now The Shaman is telling me that he and everyone else was waiting for me to be done and not the other way around. I began to change my view and trust what he was telling me but I still found it incredulous.

"*I* kept us out late?" I asked him to repeat. He didn't respond.

"After you grabbed her you still kept us in circle," he said matter-of-factly, as though we shared the same opinion. "You liked her. She was your type of gal, alright."

Don Eduardo added a rather pornographic comment about where I placed my face and obviously delighted in teasing me. My head was trying to adjust on my shoulders because I felt off-center. I only remembered wanting to complete that ceremony so badly that I was stamping my feet and constantly getting up and down to stay warm. I got out of my tent churning about the ceremony, believing I had failed. A few minutes' walk across the bowl and don Eduardo was telling me I had some things seriously backwards in my understanding. This was no joking Indian pulling my leg. He meant it, although at first I also had no idea what he meant. I finally grasped his import but I did not see how I had kept us out late until years later. I thought we were waiting for don Eduardo to finish and he said it was the other way around. Everyone was waiting on me? To be done with that light cloud, that "her" that so attracted me? Was that the truth?

I did experience some kind of conscious life force within that light cloud, and "she" was utterly mesmerizing, both indisputable facts to me. She was real enough that I perceived "her" to move entirely independent of my influence. The very notion of my having an effect on that sentient light cloud by puking on her, well how does anyone seriously take credit for such a thing? It would be many years before I could accept the proposition and realize it occurred exactly as don Eduardo reported. It's a level of consciousness distinction, and those hours at Marcawasi during ceremony with Shaman don Eduardo Calderon were like no other.

"People in your world call it luck," don Eduardo said. "Shamans call it *power*. She approached and you liked her so much you had to have her. Now you pretend to know nothing of the kind. You're a little strange but then so are we all. You could say you were lucky but it would bring you nothing," don Eduardo added. "A shaman knows that his world is a description. Remember *power* from last night and it will remember you."

By now many people were standing around listening. I recognized that don Eduardo was coaching me for how to organize my experience but at the time all I could do was hear him clearly enough to mark the conversation in my mind. I would think about it on the walk down the mountain. I did not feel like continuing the conversation, so we all turned our attention to packing up and leaving but not before we had a final circle to say goodbye to this place. Don Eduardo declared the spirit had initiated two of us, the Roshi and me, and also Lorena, "half initiated," leaving everyone to question for a long time what the heck did that mean? If anyone was a shaman among us, it was that woman and don Eduardo did fully acknowledge her a year or two later. Lorena was the only one among us who carried the shaman's mantle boldly into the public arena. She took many pilgrims on journeys around the world before she died fifteen years later. We remained close though we didn't speak often and never missed a beat when we did. Her life force never dimmed while her body took its course. Following her heart she led a bold existence with dramatic wins and losses. She left very thankful for a full life and very conscious that Home was her next and final stop. I assured her I would meet her there.

Don Eduardo left the big orange tent standing. He said the owner could come for it and meanwhile the spirits of the place would enjoy it. It was an uneventful walk down the mountain. The young people from the village went ahead of our group and by the time we arrived a number of families had prepared food.

I was sitting on the ground leaning against a stonewall slurping my bowl of soup when don Eduardo came over to me. "Randy, there's one more thing," as if we had last talked only a minute ago. "We have spoken about this before. Now you must understand. A shaman never vacates his consciousness and body entirely. If an (spirit) entity wants to communicate, you must make them sit on the mat with you face to face. Your mind and body belong only to you."

"Don Eduardo," I said, "I can't imagine why I would ever do such a thing. I make you a promise that it will never happen."

"There are great healers who allow a spirit to entirely possess them," don Eduardo added. "Our only difference is that we always keep at least one eye peeking."

At the time I believed that I understood what don Eduardo meant. We had talked enough about relationship with spirit consciousness that I understood this to be a matter of style among shamans, a kind of self-respect for your own life and identity in this world of time and space inhabiting a body. It's too precious, every moment, to give it away to another sentience who could misuse "you," and once you do, there's no way to guarantee you can have it back, according to the shamans. I had attended large events with famous channels such as Ramtha and Lazarus, and I had had firsthand experience freeing people from malicious spirit possession during ceremonies with jungle shamans in the Amazon. So the reality of the entire business was not in question for me. I could not see any reason why I would ever vacate my own identity or ever want to lend my mind and body to another entity without reserving dominion. Nothing about the idea was attractive to me so it was rather easy to make don Eduardo my promise. I was also sincere about the shaman's point of view, which at the time looked like the correct choice.

"If the spirit wants to speak to you so badly," don Eduardo added one last time, "let him sit on the mat with you face-to-face."

"Don Eduardo," I replied, "thank you for sharing with me your sacred path. My life will reflect your touch and I will always remember these times with you."

Little did I realize that one day this promise would place me at the crossroad of another initiation with enormous and conflicting choices.

CHAPTER FIVE

The Casa of Dom Inacio

Thirteen years later standing in front of a fully incorporated spiritualist medium healer.

Along the desert plateau of northern Brazil nestles a curious "village" within a small town called Abadiania. In one corner of the small town is a little spiritual hospital, which sits on a few acres next to vast ranch lands on the outskirts of town where some of the streets are paved and others are clay dirt. Horse and donkey-drawn carts clack along cobbled streets while every kind of modern vehicle passes them by. Very humble people living in modest surroundings frequently stand in their doorways to watch people from around the world walk toward the Casa, where they will stand in line with Brazilians from every walk of life. They are all there to receive spiritual healing for physical, mental and emotional conditions or simply to be in the presence of spiritual mastery. Many of the local people rely totally on this spiritual hospital for all their medical and spiritual needs while others ignore the place entirely and think it's all a hoax.

The little hospital is called Casa de Dom Inacio (the House of Ignatius Loyola) after the signatory spirit in charge of all healing activity. A single person, a spiritualist medium, supported by many volunteers, offers free healing to all who come. Authentic healing sometimes occurs right on the spot with a complete cure and full restitution, be it physical, mental, emotional, or spiritual. Whatever the condition, there's a documented track record of it having happened one or more times. This is not to say that everyone leaves cured and healed, nor does anyone make such a claim, but in my experience most are helped if not healed and report the same.

Known affectionately around the world as Joao de Deus ("John of God"), this Brazilian spiritualist medium treats everyone who arrives at the Casa of Dom Inacio. His given name is Joao Teixeiria de Faria and he is the most powerful full-trance medium healer in the world. At least that is the opinion of many who know about these things. In his trance he willingly and intentionally becomes entirely unconscious, vacating his mind and body to allow a spirit referred to as "Entity" to entirely take over. The Entity Consciousness that takes possession of Joao's mind and body sometimes has abilities that are clearly paranormal. On a previous visit to the Casa, Joao's Entity healed me of a debilitating injury without physically touching my body. A hernia that required imminent surgery for standard repair disappeared in forty-five minutes of sitting in prayer session with the Entity occupying the body of Joao, the medium.

There are only a handful of spiritualist mediums world-renowned for their accomplishments and demonstrations, and Joao Teixieria de Faria of Brazil, known as Joao de Deus, is rightly at the top of anyone's list.

Joao is the very kind of person Shaman don Eduardo had told me dwells in the world at any given time and who meets the ancient Inca criteria to qualify as "a Shaman of the South," a healer with extraordinary abilities. Not only did I meet a healer who satisfied the ancient criteria of the Incas, and gain some modest admittance into the personal world of the medium Joao, but I also made deep contact with several of the thirty or more spirits whom he incorporates. Some are known historical figures, such as Ignatius Loyola, the supposed founder and patron saint of the Jesuit priesthood within the Catholic Church while others are medical doctors from the last century such as Doctors Augusto Almeida and Oswaldo Cruz. Both doctors were well known in Brazilian circles when they were alive in bodies and for the past century these beings, along with many others, have worked closely with the Brazilian spiritualist community. Many of the entities are not recognized, historically or otherwise, and have not offered much information about their physical lives, preferring instead to simply treat people and only talk about what the patient needs to get well. The Entities that manifest through Joao's mind and body are dissimilar in personality and appearance, which is evident in Joao's physical demeanor while an Entity is present. Each Entity's presence is distinct, sometimes holy or profound, sometimes strangely beneficent, sometimes quiet and steady, and oftentimes powerful. Although witnessing these incorporated entities is sometimes confusing and difficult to decide how one feels, it is still a positive experience. It's the "real deal," as contemporary slang would say.

I stood in the middle of a long line of people dressed mostly in white clothing, which is the custom when visiting the Casa. The line slowly flowed, one by one, through a small door at the far end of the little auditorium. I had been to this spiritual hospital on several previous visits to this central high desert of Brazil, waiting my turn in line to speak face-to-face with a four-hundred-year-old spirit. On this day the medium and his entities would bring me to an excruciating threshold of tension regarding the promise I made to Shaman don Eduardo Calderon years earlier: that I would never release myself *entirely* to a spirit and would always retain recognition of my own identity. It had been years since I had even considered the possibility, yet on this day the shaman's *nagual* seeped through the fabric of time and influenced another kind of initiation I was about to face. There would be no San Pedro to empower me to leave my mind behind and no ceremonial protocols to guide my actions except a promise I had made to Shaman don Eduardo that final day at Marcawasi. Now its full portent that I had never realized was about to land in my lap with consequences that could not be escaped.

The Medium Joao rolled his eyes back and vacated his body to give it over entirely to the spirit entity that now accepted full admission into his corporeal form. The eyes that opened were different. We all look very different at times but seldom entirely different for a sustained period except when we are ill or medicated. During ceremony and ritual or even simple church practices, we sometimes show up looking and being different from our normal appearance. Joao's change when he incorporated an entity was of an entirely different magnitude. It wasn't just a different look; it was a different person looking out at me. The animation of the body was different than the medium's. The hair looked straighter and longer and hung differently. The slope of the shoulders, the hang of the jaw, the torso and full body torque and movement, the vocabulary and accent, the way the face muscles organized, it all changed. Sometimes even his eye color changed.

"So what do you do?" the Entity sitting in the chair asked me.

I was standing before the fully incorporated medium and the spirit speaking through him. For hours I had been waiting in a slowly and steadily moving line that wound its way through praying and meditating people. Many people got a second or two in front of him before he dispensed a communication and moved on to the next person. Many had more substantial exchanges though mostly they were extremely brief, and always with many people within listening distance. Loud contemplative music from an assortment of speakers offered some amount of privacy. Usually the audience would stand at least a few feet back but there was never any complete privacy. Whatever you had to say, whatever had brought you, and whatever would occur would be thoroughly witnessed by more than a few. Quite understandably, sometimes people have nothing to say before Entity and simply receive with gratitude whatever he has for them.

On this occasion I had come to seek direct engagement with the Entity at a spiritual training level and I was having that exact thought looking at him. Before I spoke the words to my translator, the Entity said, as though he had heard my thoughts, "I understand" (*eo intendo*) and then asked again with an enchanting and wry smile, "Tell me what you do."

My mind raced to find a simple and clear phrasing that would communicate directly and quickly since I spoke very little Portuguese and was using a translator. While I spoke to the translator, the Entity interrupted and spoke again. "I know why you are here," the Entity said pointedly. "I want you to tell me, I want to hear what you say. What do you do?"

The look from the Entity reminded me of a professor who sees an answer hanging nearby and wants you to grab it. But how do I say what I do? I had come there to fulfill something I had been working on for years. How do I say that? I asked myself. "I work with energy," I finally said while looking the Entity in the eyes.

A deadpan serious look dramatically came over his face followed by a strange, wide-eyed grin, which left me uncertain whether I had said the correct or incorrect magic words. The Entity looked up at the translator who had a similar strange look on his face. I could see that I had touched something but I had no idea what. The Entity leaned forward from his chair in a most deliberate manner and looked me over very seriously but with a kind smile while his jutting chin followed his stare from my feet to my crown. It was slightly unnerving, and I had a distinct feeling that something tangible was probing my mind and body. I felt utterly naked in front of this being. While I entirely welcomed and trusted him, his visual examination was also raw and point-blank, both extremely personal and utterly impersonal at the same time. It was likely how many of us feel on the doctor's table undressed and being probed. You accept it but you're not sure you like it.

"What do you want of me?" the Entity asked, leaning his elbow on the chair and looking me squarely in the face. "I know why you are here and I want you to tell me."

"I want your assistance to direct energy with my intentions," I replied.

"Will you heal with it?" the Entity asked. I was momentarily flustered by the quickness of his question, but before I could answer he continued, "Because if you won't heal then I won't give you energy."

I was surprised at first by his strong, immediate response with a question I had not anticipated. Healing anyone was not what I had on my mind with my energy statement. I instantly flashed on why he might be saying that to me. There had been several times in my life where I had caused my own body to change rather rapidly, and through this change I was able to affect other people with substantial results. But on each occasion something dramatic had spontaneously occurred under unusual circumstances. I had never forgotten these experiences but I had been very reluctant to claim that I had healed anyone and much more inclined to follow the shaman's predilection: conduct the ritual and accept the results. In other words, if it worked and someone improved ostensibly from your ministering, credit something beyond yourself for the result while acknowledging your own part.

"I am not a healer who holds myself out that way in the world," I started to say when the Entity interrupted me rather sharply.

"Answer my question," the Entity demanded loudly and sternly. "Will you heal with it? If yes, I will give you energy, otherwise I won't. What do you want?"

Wow. This guy means business, in my face, point blank, wanting to know whether I'm a player in his game. I have been to this corridor before where every word and gesture has consequences. I approached expecting some lofty or meditative blessing and instead there's someone over there demanding to know with some precision who is over here. Humm. What did I expect?

"Yes," I said, "I will gratefully heal with it but I am not someone who will hang out a sign about it."

"Will you at least heal when the Spirit asks that of you?" the Entity inquired more patiently. "I will give you energy if you will heal when you are asked to do so."

"Yes," I replied, "I would humbly heal and offer energy whenever the Spirit asks that of me."

I knew I was being truthful and sincere with my answer yet a very uncomfortable feeling ran through me. Had I just one more time with one more spiritual master made a promise with consequences more than I bargained for? I did not have time to complete the thought while the energy ran along my neck with an electric feeling.

"Very well then," he abruptly said, surprisingly loudly and rather dramatically in a rapid tone shift I did not expect.

Again looking straight into my eyes, with a sense of penetration into my inner world, he said, "Come this afternoon and I will test you." Then he looked over my shoulder to the next person in line, signaling my time was over and leaving me not a moment in his presence to respond further.

I followed my translator Martin outside to discuss what had just happened. Martin is an exceptional person with a quiet dignity and sensitivity to people that made him very comfortable to be around in this complex environment. He runs one of the more popular international pousadas (usually a simple motel that offers a room and serves meals) in "the village," meaning the part of Abadiania close to the Casa. He is a caring friend to Medium Joao and volunteers his time assisting at the Casa and translating in several languages for the myriad travelers who arrive there.

"Martin, why did he say that to me?" I asked. "What does he mean, 'I will test you?' And test me about what?" I asked as though I had not a clue what he meant while deep inside I felt a rumbling for his meaning.

"You have used words that are somewhat notorious at the Casa, but I have never seen the Entity react that way," Martin replied.

"What kind of words do you mean?" I asked him.

"Many times people come to the Casa and tell the Entity they work with energy," Martin answered. "The Entity usually tells them otherwise or tells them to go and pray. I have no idea what the Entity means to test you about but the afternoon will come soon enough and you will find out."

"Look, Martin," I explained, starting to get a little concerned, *"working with energy* is a very specific shorthand for many of my activities where energy, spiritual energy, is at the heart of the matter. I expected the Entity to see what I meant and I assume that he did. Yes, I work with energy alright, but I certainly don't go around offering to heal people and never meant to imply that I do!"

I must have looked and sounded more concerned than I realized.

"No, no, it's alright," Martin interrupted, responding to my agitation and now wanting to reassure me. "I'm sure the Entity understood you perfectly. You worked with Carlos Castaneda and the Entity remembers the jungle shaman you told him about last time you were here. Don't you remember that? He said that you are protected from black magic and not to worry. Yes, he remembers you. I think it's good, and very interesting. This afternoon we will ask him what he means. No?"

I was surprised that Martin remembered so much detail from a conversation a year earlier since he translates for dozens of people every session. His tone was very reassuring but it also made me appreciate that I was more on his radar than I realized. I had spoken to the Entity about disturbing dreams of encounters I had had in the desert in Peru while helping a jungle shaman protect don Eduardo from a jealous group of sorcerers. Subsequent to that participation I found myself questioning whether I was at risk from the same jungle shaman who wanted me to learn more about his methods than I cared to. From time to time I became concerned whether I had escaped unscathed and Martin reminded me of what the Entity had said to me. Even though it had been years since helping to protect don Eduardo after he had been viciously attacked and almost killed, it was a tremendous relief being told I need not worry about black magic affecting me. The entity told me that I never had any malice in my heart and no tendrils back to me existed from those days. I also remembered the ridiculous story Martin had heard about how Carlos Castaneda died in a supernatural manner. I had explained to him that Carlos died in a body like everyone else, although highly conscious that he was passing, and Martin thought (correctly) that was a great accomplishment. I remembered that point was especially meaningful to Martin.

I presumed from Martin's comments that I would get in line again during afternoon session, and when my turn came I could ask the Entity what he wanted to test me about. The Entity had a serious deadpan stare that left no doubt he took the matter seriously enough for me to feel the gravity around it. While I was absolutely serious myself, it appeared that the Entity had perceived me to mean something more specific than I realized. Test me about what? I kept asking myself. Even though the question weighed heavily in my thoughts and feelings, I trusted Joao de Deus and the sentience that occupied his body. I had by this time seen him perform quite a number of seemingly miraculous healings, asking nothing in return. Whatever he meant I was willing to find out, although I felt on edge, like scheduled to perform for a major occasion and not knowing what exactly.

When I went back to my room to lie down during the midday break, I was filled with memories of my journeys with Shaman don Eduardo Calderon. I was not trying to think about these memories but they continued to flood my thoughts, such as our time at Marcawasi, the unbelievable adventures that followed and the reasons why I had abandoned the identity of shaman as a formal pursuit. In Peru I did not enjoy the competitive notoriety that mantle attracted, and in my own American culture I had concluded that it was a counterproductive identification since it required such an extraordinary fabric of relationships among people who shared specific and common assumptions about existence. There could be no shamans who didn't live on Indian reservations. In other words, a shaman is a person by blood and by culture bound to a tradition and a group of people with recent indigenous ancestry and thereby exchanges certain bonds and obligations to that community. Shamans created in Western psycho-spiritual workshops are something entirely different.

In the past twenty years there's been an explosion of workshops offering to train anyone who signs up to be a shaman. A shaman might become a dancer, a drummer, a soul retriever, or a workshop leader. While all these activities are exceedingly meritorious in their own right, with many excellent practitioners, they bore little resemblance to my own experiences. Not to say anything was wrong or incorrect so much as simply not a lot that I recognized. Within a very short time in our popular understanding, being a shaman took on new meaning. Originally a shaman was a person *initiated* by a culturally sanctioned shaman and thereby transformed into a rare kind of person who was mystical and practical in nature. The shaman from prehistoric lineages bore the responsibility of maintaining the living link between everyday life and active awareness of the spiritual. It was the responsibility of the shaman to uphold *as a living demonstration* the reality of *senior spiritual identity*. The shaman's life was his or her demonstration of their connecting link with The Spirit. That demonstration can appear in a variety of ways, depending upon the person and the times.

Personally, I have identified more with the intentions of the *nagual* sorcerers, who pursue their own illumination within a band of cherished cohorts and neither resist nor bow to the times they live in while purposefully concerning themselves with lofty pursuits. As for healing, the shamans I have most identified with say take care of it when it's needed in whatever manner is necessary and certainly work primarily with energy.

I remembered when don Eduardo had told me that during the time of the Incas only a certain kind of shaman would ever declare himself to be a healer, a Shaman of The South, which he considered himself to be. He joked with me that he would have been killed off early in his career since he claimed that an Incan shaman had three days to accept or decline any request to heal, and if he (or she) refused a healing request very often, the community would lose faith. Upon the third day, if not sooner, the shaman had to act, keeping in mind that *the penalty for failing to completely restore the patient was death.* At the time I took don Eduardo to be purposefully exaggerating but he insisted it was true and made no claim to such ability himself. He said there were others in the world with such ability. He didn't think anyone could do it all the time, every time, and that's why even the Inca master shamans could sometimes refuse a healing request.

I remembered my promise to don Eduardo that I would never incorporate a spirit Entity, such as what I had witnessed the Medium Joao doing. I wholeheartedly admired what I saw Joao doing, but I had not the slightest desire to be like him. I considered it a very rare and privileged gift from God, exactly as Joao did, and in no way did I compare my own talents with this man's extraordinary abilities. At a technical level I also considered what Joao did to be very dangerous and a special assignment. After all, even Medium Joao never sought his vocation, it just started happening to him. I deeply respected mediums and mediumship but did not share the confidence of many that it was easy to avoid undesirable spirits entering and exiting trance. Once another being possesses your body and faculties, it's too late to question their integrity. That was the traditional concern and danger for these shamans, who had many times shown me good reason to take that caution seriously. Minimally, you better know for darn certain who you are inviting in, and how does one do that?

The first time I went to the Casa of Dom Inacio, I did not automatically trust in the Entity since my study of history placed the Jesuits at the forefront of the nefarious Catholic Inquisition during and after the Renaissance. The first time I had the chance I asked the incorporated Entity, none other than Ignatius Loyola, how he could have been involved in such a horror, since history identifies the Jesuits of the Spanish Inquisition as having conducted some of the most grotesque crimes against humanity imaginable. I seriously needed an answer. I was sincerely humbled by his spontaneous and peaceful reply, done with candor, thoroughness and absolute certainty. He told me lucid detail as though he were there of the events at the end of his life in the sixteenth century Spain. Speaking to me as Ignatius Loyola, who was alive at the time, he told me the Pope had ordered him confined to house arrest the last fifteen years of his life. He would have been killed if he had tried to leave and while he did not fear death, he wanted to serve the people with a living reminder to place their trust in God. He had become a spiritual leader and was organizing to found an order of priests *who would singularly follow the teachings of Jesus and remain apart from Vatican politics or control.* Because too many priests wanted to follow his lead and it was threatening to the establishment the authorities took notice and the Pope ordered him restrained. "But God had other plans for me," he wistfully sighed.

Because of his wide-ranging popularity, throngs of people regularly came to visit him and in the last ten years of his life God gave him the gift of healing, which he accomplished for countless visitors, curing many by the touch of his hand. This arrangement worked very well politically for the church, because it appeared that Ignatius Loyola and the church were on the same team. For Loyola the politics no longer mattered since God had arranged for him to minister to as many people as he could see in spite of his confinement. After he died, the church formed the order of the Jesuits and capitalized on his name and reputation and claiming Loyola had founded it. He told me that he had had nothing to do with the formation of the Jesuit order and had never been a participant. No wonder the modern Catholic Church condemns and attacks Joao de Deus, but not all of the membership, far from it! On my last visit to the Casa there were three Jesuit priests who came to honor and pray with Dom Inacio, the very same Ignatius Loyola purported to have founded their order. All three of them went onto the stage, likely in defiance of current papal orders, and acknowledged The Entity Dom Inacio as being fully incorporated by Joao de Deus kneeling before him and kissing his hand. What a precious, pious and wondrous union in forgiveness and blessing for all concerned and abundantly clear that not everyone in the Catholic hierarchy agreed with the party line.

As I lay on my bed, I realized I was playing these thoughts about entities over and over again in my head, so I paused to take another look. Why was I thinking about entities taking over a person's body and mind? Was I feeling a conflict about that promise to don Eduardo? I had not formally practiced the shaman's path for a number of years although I had entirely upheld the sacredness of the craft within my private spiritual practices. I completely honored what I saw in Joao de Deus and the entities working through him, so what was the problem? I did not feel any personal attraction toward becoming a medium who incorporated spirits, or did I? I certainly did not want to be a healer with a shingle, although I had served a similar function much of my adult life working as a therapist and personal coach. In no way did I consider myself as someone who restored sick people as the basis for my offer to the world. I had purposefully completed my work as a therapist and at this time in my life I chose to work with healthy people, while fully appreciating it was all subjective and relative. That thought grabbed me with an uncomfortable edge. Why did I even need to make a judgment about sick or healthy folks and instead simply follow my own heart?

After twenty years I had become very clear about the limitations and constraints the professional therapist counselor role dictated. I was weary of the administrative requirements to only offer solutions that served the needs of control organizations more than the person seeking assistance. At the same time self-indulgence and simple lack of personal discipline was often the source of too many people's problems, and that's not really a clinical matter, or even a psychotherapy issue. The so called human potential movement roaring up out of the sixties and seventies offered countless venues that better served people's growth and development than most therapy models, at least ones controlled by licensing laws and self serving professional organizations. I did not agree with being required to place a diagnosis in people's records given all the mischief such labels cause in people's lives. Boredom and a sense of missing out on life's rewards is a very frequent malaise in relationships, and the courage to climb out of that hole is considerable. It also provides a reason to visit counselors and help always depends on willingness to change and that's normally not easy for any of us. Usually I was able to help anyone who truly wanted help, but that also required some degree of attitude change from them and frequently of their personal habits. Help and healing is always always synonymous with change, real change, and nothing in between. In this exact same breath from my professional experience with thousands of people I fully realized that the same would be true for me if I wanted to receive whatever Dom Inacio had in store for me. My attitude and my willingness to change would certainly matter, of that I was certain. I drifted in my thoughts until it was time to walk back to the Casa for the afternoon session.

The little open-air auditorium was packed with people so I leaned on a back wall only to look up to see Martin coming toward me. He grabbed me by the arm and we wound our way through the crowd to stand directly in front of the little stage where the incorporated Joao sometimes begins sessions performing public surgeries to give witness to those assembled. Physical, on the flesh, surgery most often must be specifically requested but the Entity does not always accept, and may advise prayer and lifestyle changes instead. That should not surprise anyone who has investigated their own inner world with some degree of sustained discipline. We recognize within ourselves that for lasting change to occur in our physical health then complementary attitudinal change also needs to occur and neither is complete without the other.

"This should be good," Martin said with a subtle edge of excited anticipation that gave me the feeling that he was tracking my reactions carefully and enjoying himself in the process.

"I have never seen the Entity want to test anyone," Martin said, belying a subtle pleasure he was taking watching my reactions to his comments.

I was not sure how to interpret Martin. There was a certain tone of playful mischief in his remark that made me uncomfortable. I felt he knew more than he was saying and clearly he was enjoying watching me deal with the ambiguity. We both still said that we would simply get in line after the public surgeries to ask The Entity what he wanted to test me about. To tell the truth, even I did not believe that but at the same time I truly had no idea what to expect and did not foresee what was about to happen.

On this day I was barely aware of the speakers and buried deeply in my own thoughts when I looked up to see the Medium Joao step onto the little stage. The speaker stopped talking in mid-sentence and left the stage. It was quickly obvious that the Medium Joao was himself and had not incorporated an Entity. Joao escorted a man onto the stage with him and the entire room went silent as they stood before us.

"Good afternoon, my brothers and sisters," Joao said. "We are honored this day to have a special medium visiting us who will conduct our afternoon healing session."

Joao explained that one of the most famous and powerful full incorporation medium healers from the south of Brazil had just paid him a visit. Upon learning how famous and powerful this man was, Joao told his audience that he felt he should honor this healer by letting him commence our healing session. I heard an unusual agitation in Joao's voice that conveyed something incongruous within his words. Another time I had seen a similarly agitated look on the medium's face when he yelled at some taxi drivers because they had overcharged some gullible Americans for local rides to the Casa. Soon rates were posted in all the cabs or they could not come to the Casa to wait for fares. The Medium Joao cared very much about the many details that comprised the operation and flow of the Casa, so his offer to sponsor another healer to conduct the session was rather extraordinary. The Catholic Church and the

Brazilian medical society frequently sued him or tried to have him arrested. The Church believed that only they can sponsor Ignatius Loyola, whom they count among their saints, and the medical society universally demands a sole legal monopoly to "cure the sick," even though they are considerably less successful than Joao. Likely that's the rub, because they know it. Joao performs more operations in a single day than most hospitals in a month. Worst of all for traditional medicine, he charges nothing. Joao has successfully treated many people in government who have helped to create laws to protect him. Out of the thousands (some claim millions) treated by Joao, rarely has anyone complained about treatment. The Church and the Brazilian legal medical authorities have pounced on the few cases where people claimed they were not helped or damaged. Consequently, it was no small matter for Joao to invite another healer to conduct the session.

"Let us all now say the 'Our Father' prayer to support this medium to incorporate," Joao requested.

Whenever Joao prepared to incorporate an entity in the auditorium, he usually asked for everyone to pray out loud, so initially it seemed like he was honoring his guest. Since Joao was standing directly in front of me and only a few feet away, I could also hear him speak to this man. "Incorporate now and let us see you heal," Joao said sharply and deliberately. "I'll give you a couple of minutes to do it." Then he began the prayer and we all chorused along.

"Martin," I whispered, "who is this man?"

"I don't know," he replied, "I have never heard of him."

"What?" I asked. "Then why does Joao want him to conduct the healing session?"

"I don't know," Martin whispered back. "I have been here eight years and he has never asked anyone else to heal on the stage. This must be someone very powerful or Medium Joao would not present him to us."

What a profound opportunity, I thought, to be able to witness yet another healing maestro in action working with Joao de Deus. The thought was staggering and for a moment I thought I was about to watch a rare treat and something I had never even heard of let alone witnessed, a visiting incorporating medium working with another incorporating medium. Wow. While the entire gathering spoke the prayer, we all watched the guest healer. We were probably expecting him to roll back his eyes and go into a trance, much the way we had seen Joao do many times. Instead, the man became bug-eyed and stood there transfixed, as though frozen in place. At first I thought it was the usual bizarre look mediums sometimes take on while entering or exhibiting trance. But I was immediately confused because I could not see anything peaceful emanating from the so-called healer. He had his hands clasped in front of himself so tightly they were turning white and red. Mediums in trance usually don't cross their hands or legs during trance because it grounds the energy to their own body personality identity and energy systems when that is exactly what they are attempting to release to inter-dimensional influence and control. The man was also perspiring profusely with sweat pouring down his temples, and it was not particularly hot. His face looked like a dazed deer in front of headlights, frozen with fear, and he was having a difficult time breathing.

Joao paced back and forth behind him, looking impatient and very concerned. Then he abruptly walked up to the man and spoke in a low, strong voice. "I'll give you another twenty seconds to incorporate and begin healing, or get off the stage," Joao ordered and began pacing again.

The man's breathing became labored and a look of terror chiseled his face. He appeared unable to move while a thousand people stared at him. Joao walked back to him and began speaking to us while the man remained motionless in drenched clothing. "This man insisted on visiting me," Joao sternly spoke to the audience, "and told me that he does what I do. He said in the south of Brazil he is a famous full incorporation medium and he heals just like I do. I thought it only proper that he perform some of the healing today."

Joao began pacing again and by now the meaning was clear that this man was not who he had said he was and Joao was treating him to a rather brutal lesson. Amazed, I wondered what kind of person would put himself in such an exposed and vulnerable position so as to guarantee utter humiliation. Somehow sheer stupidity was hardly enough to fully explain such a pathetic blunder.

Joao stopped pacing and impatiently faced the man. "Leave the stage," he ordered. "We must begin our session. There are many here who need my help."

Without waiting for a reply, Joao clenched his fists, rolled his eyes back and staggered for a few moments, almost falling down. Two house mediums assisting Joao when in trance rushed forward to hold him while Joao vacated his body. The famous incorporation guest medium on the stage remained motionless, paralyzed without much awareness of what was taking place right next to him. Slowly Joao raised his head and stood up straight and it was clear that an entirely different animation now filled his body. At first he moved in slow motion, as if he were trying on his new suit and then he settled into the body as though he suddenly recognized it. He gave the impression of being taller and thinner than before. The presence was older, regal, and very serene. Everyone felt it, a complete contrast to the emphatic and agitated medium speaking to us only a minute before. A subtle golden opaque light shined from nowhere onto the stage while profound peace and authority emanated from this being.

He raised his hand with the index finger pointing up and spoke a blessing to those on the stage. Hushed whispers and excitement rustled among some in the audience while the sound of "Dom Inacio" rustled around the auditorium. The Entity slowly turned and looked directly into the eyes of the various people standing along the wall at the back of the stage. Several people quickly walked up and kneeled before him, kissing his hand with tearful joy. With an air of authority and dignity, he blessed them as they thanked the signatory spirit in charge of the Casa for visiting. By now the entire auditorium was totally focused on the Entity as he turned and walked to face us at the front of the stage.

"My dear children, many people come to this house of God," Dom Inacio said, "and tell the Medium Joao they heal like he does. They often say *they work with energy*. He knows they do not and tells them to go and pray. The Medium is worried that you could be delayed in finding your healing if you do not know how to distinguish those who heal from those who don't. He wants you to know how to tell the difference."

When I heard Dom Inacio use the term, energy, I silently groaned to myself and instantly assumed this was the lesson and the test for me. Somehow I had to reframe and find more exacting words for saying what it was that I did, although in the moment, in spite of feeling self-conscious about it, I affirmed to myself that I did work with energy and meant what I said.

Then Dom Inacio turned to the guest, who was still frozen like a statue. He gently placed his arms around him as though he were thawing him out and tenderly spoke to him with a most compassionate voice and caring manner. "My son, my son, don't you realize that you could have harmed yourself?" he tenderly asked. "If you want to learn to heal you should approach the Medium and ask for his help. He will help if you ask but you must not lie to him." Holding the man by his shoulders, he turned him around and the disoriented guest wobbled toward the back of the stage. "Now go and lean on that wall and watch and learn," he said as he gently pushed him toward the back wall where the man nearly collapsed against it.

Dom Inacio then turned and walked to the front of the stage and spoke again with a booming and all business kind of voice as though a larger and serious drama had begun. "Now there are also people who come to the Casa that do work with energy," he told us. "You, this man, he is such a one. Come forward," Dom Inacio declared as he pointed most emphatically into the audience.

For a moment I looked over my shoulder to see the person Dom Inacio pointed to as he walked from the center of the stage directly toward me. Seeing instead many faces staring back at me, I turned around and realized his eyes were looking directly into mine. He gestured imperatively for me to come and kneel in front of him on the concrete stage. This I did immediately and he told me very quickly in an almost brusque command to extend my hands and to enter trance. In a moment I was kneeling like an altar boy with my hands extended straight out in front of me at eye level. Without having any idea what exactly he wanted me to do, I simply let go and sent my consciousness to a place I had acquainted myself with over many years. I can only go there under pressure or during ceremony, it's a part of shamanism I have retained and practiced. It's a place so deep and real that inner reality predominates, even though I can be tangentially aware of the outer environment in contact with my body.

Energy arrives, a kind of energy that vibrates through me with sufficient intensity to alter my physical potentials. At the Casa it's called *current* and it was palpable and intense, giving me strength and stillness. My being still organized itself around the ten percent rule given by the shamans: to retain enough self-referential identity to be aware of it while inviting spiritual forces to cohabitate my inner reality. Of course I wasn't thinking about any such thing, I was just letting go into the deepest inner reality I could access under the circumstances. I went inwardly very deep, to be sure, but I knew who I was and where I was, although I had only a distant sense of the outer environment. In that state of trance, I could kneel effortlessly on concrete as if suspended on guy wires but from time to time Dom Inacio's movement and sounds were so alluring they would snag my attention. Imagine a four-hundred-year-old "saint" manifesting healing one after another on the stage right next to you. Dom Inacio does not incorporate very often at the Casa and people who have come to The Casa for many years to sit in *current* with Joao told me that normally he does not speak a lot. History and high holy healing were taking place all around me and there was no way I could not feel it penetrating my inner world. It could be extremely demanding in those moments to remain deep and not go external. Soon, however, I took myself deeper and deeper into the *current* that flowed through me like a warm sacred wind steadily soothing me. Soon the *current* became substantial enough to hold me securely without effort. I completely let go into it.

For twenty minutes I remained in that kneeling position, eyes closed with arms outstretched, my mind in a very deep trance. Sometimes my inner sight would go external without opening my eyes and I could see rapid scenes of the activity going on around me. During that time Dom Inacio called people out of the audience and healed people of many conditions right there, on the spot. One young man had just incurred a nasty sprain and possible broken foot only hours before the session. It was black and blue and swollen like a balloon but completely normal by the time the session was over. Dom Inacio called a medical doctor and longtime cohort of mine to the stage to witness and suture some of the almost instant physical surgeries, which he performed with medical instruments while the patient stood on the stage. No anesthesia was used and rarely was there much blood, nor did the patient appear to feel pain; a shirt or pants would be pulled back just enough to cut into the body at the needed location. Tumors and body mass, quickly excised with precise skill, would get tossed on the floor or on a tray.

Finally, Dom Inacio walked over to me and pushed on my arms that were effortlessly rigid in front of me but strongly buoyant, as if tied to balloons. Pushing again at the spring in my hands, he told me to open my eyes. My doctor friend whom Dom Inacio had pulled from the audience was standing next to me.

Rather dramatically, Dom Inacio broke open a surgical pack and showed me what he was taking out. Slowly he pulled a piece of glistening steel from a paper package, a large 14-gauge catheter needle, the kind they use to suck fluids into and out of the body. It's a little thicker than a round toothpick. At the time I had no idea what it was and learned this later. It had a green wrap on one end for a handle. Again he pushed on my arms, smiling as if he enjoyed feeling their buoyancy and the energy running out my hands. "Are you afraid?" he asked.

"No," I said, "I'm not afraid."

I was very surprised to hear my own voice. It answered before I could think about it. Literally. As far as I recognized myself, I was not able to talk because I could not find the faculty to do so in that trance state, but clearly someone answered him. I had no thoughts let alone any idea what he was going to do with the surgical instrument he held before me. One time at Jack Schwarz' Alethia Foundation I had demonstrated on their instruments, verbalizing to Jack's wife Lois while exhibiting a delta state brain wave or the state when one is normally in deep sleep. It's possible that I was in a delta brain wave condition because I could only see a couple of feet around me and nothing beyond. Whatever my actual brain wave condition, I was about as deep as I could be and still be able to remain present in the moment, the ten percent that rarely verbalized.

Dom Inacio stood directly in front of me and lifted my outstretched hand such that I was looking up at a line of sight across the top of my hand and directly into his eyes while he took the 14-gauge catheter needle and slowly pressed it into the back of my right hand until it pushed against the palm flesh like a pencil tip. There was no blood. I felt the needle as if it were a low-grade burn, the way that candle wax burns just enough to make it a real choice how it feels as I watched it go into my hand. For a split second I had a lucid flash of another time and another man watching his hand being pierced. It could have hurt on one channel in my mind while on another it made no difference. It was nothing except glorious, partly as an act of steel mental discipline but mostly because it was utterly compelling to reside there. My mind was electric, silent, and fierce with intention. I was razor sharp with my focus, ninety percent released entirely to the moment and just enough of "me" to fully realize what was happening. It was sublime, ecstatic and pure, at least for a few moments, until suddenly a man ran up to take pictures and the flash went off directly in my face. And he kept taking pictures!

I discovered later that he was Sebastian, a cosmic co-conspirator in all of this though I did not know with whom or why at the time. He was Joao's oldest and closest friend, a rotund little cherub of a man known as the Casa secretary or the person who moved around the Casa *making sure everything was the way it was supposed to be*. It was an impossible job and yet he performed it perfectly and beyond anything I easily understood. I've personally seen him roll his eyes back and let entities run his mind for a few moments to write spiritual herbal prescriptions to cover for Joao, and then rush off to take a telephone call from someone needing *current* from the Entity for an emergency. Throughout the sessions he moved around assisting with whatever things needed to be taken care of. For many years he had taken photos of dramatic moments at the Casa, but I knew none of this at the time.

Like a blur coming into focus, I was forced to see this crazy fellow hovering near my face with his camera flashing until finally he succeeded in jerking my thinking mind awake. No doubt my mental reflex was exacerbated by the fact that I had not allowed my picture to be taken in many years. Oftentimes I had an unpleasant attitude about it since I did not like having my picture taken and considered it outrageously presumptive to take someone's photo without asking. With so many people taking photos during the auditorium session, I had already accepted that I would probably be in someone's picture album back home, so I had to let it go. But I had never anticipated someone running up and placing a camera a few feet from my face during some of the most spiritually intimate moments imaginable. As far as I'm concerned it's worse than someone taking suggestive photos when you are unawares. I was so deep in trance I didn't flinch or even blink at the rapid flashes, but when my conversational mind reacted that was the beginning of hell. I could no longer purely hold the deeper trance where not much more than ten percent was normal awareness. My awareness became more like forty percent, still very deep but now punctuated with awareness of people and movement around me.

"What am I doing here, what is expected?" and so on my self-reflexive mind asked itself.

I entered a condition in which heaven or hell totally engulfed my being and sometimes collided to present me with a choice. If I dwelled in my mental talk even a moment, my emotions escalated to an alarm condition that took me away from the deeper trance. I could empty my mind when I realized I needed to, but now it was work to accomplish and required energy. Finally I needed *to act* upon Dom Inacio's instructions. I could only trust the moment and for that I had to stay in the moment, the exact here and now with a silent mind. But I was not entirely silent and was finding it elusive to hold the *current* to do or be, what?

"Stand up," Dom Inacio ordered and turned me by the shoulders to face the audience.

He took my hand and pulled the catheter needle out while watching my face that did not flinch or look away. Then he placed the heels of his palms over my eye sockets and vigorously rubbed my eyes over and over. When he took his hands away I perceived a different reality than a minute before. He moved me to face the audience and I looked out at a sea of people appearing as a lattice of light and feelings looking back at me. Everyone was an explosion of energy and feelings and light and multi levels of abstract appearance. At one perfectly clear level was a pond of people looking like an audience. Overlaid onto the same scene were many textures of light emanating from and through every person as though everyone was a celluloid-like transparency that shines and transmits various colors and patterns of light.

"Now *see* the person The Spirit asks you to heal and tell me who it is," he said while holding me for a few moments as if to steady me to face the crowd.

My inner dialogue went wild. "What am I doing here? He wants me to *see* . . . what?"

The forty-percent of "me" was alive and well all right, and starting to feel threatened. I stopped my mind once again, vacating all internal dialog to such a depth of being that it produced an overwhelming and utterly lucid sight. The entire energy body, the luminous cocoon of every person before me became utterly distinct and equally discernible to the physical body. It was like seeing everyone had different kinds of spotlights inside their clothes where various levels of transparency were produced. I could literally see physical bodies as though I was looking at an x-ray and the combined effect was a cacophony of light, shading and color. It would have been an utterly sublime experience under any other circumstances. But I was not asked to enjoy what I perceived, rather to discern the mark of The Spirit on a particular person and to report what I saw. My conscious mind kept demanding to know what it was supposed to look for, and then found the question could not be answered and would become threatened not knowing what to do. Silence was my only recourse and I went back and forth for an unbearable few minutes. Standing there, probably looking dazed, I panned the people watching me, not knowing what I was looking for while being able to see virtually everything. I saw dark spots on people's organs and bones, I saw sadness, grief and a range of emotions draped on people though I cannot easily say how, except it was visual and psychic. I saw some people's joy and innocence and deep spirituality, which was in contrast to most of the audience, who had much more shallow states of being, but what I saw was a visual experience and not possible to understand. The intense overlap of every person's energy body, however, made it very difficult to discern where anything began or ended. Literally. Everyone's energy slurped onto everyone else's in this near shoulder to shoulder packed environment and my language mind kept concerning itself with that fact.

"How do I *see the person* he asks me to heal when I see so many needing healing?" my own voice demanded of me. Then I felt fear again and lost focus with the people until I forced my mind to silence. When silent I could see anyone individually but I had

157

no answers to quench the other part of my mind with its questions. I could see people with multi level clarity but it would start to fade as soon as I engaged mental dialogue. It was excruciating because, like all of us, my own voice can be absolutely compelling.

Finally Dom Inacio walked over to me, brushed against my shoulder with his shoulder and whispered to me, "Find the one with the yellow ray over his shoulder."

An involuntary feeling I did not understand went through me when he gave me his instruction. My forty-percent mind continued to scan the audience looking for a yellow ray and immediately complained from seeing bands of yellow going in every direction. I knew exactly what he meant by a "ray" but I couldn't decide who it was because I was seeing everyone's rays through everyone else's energy fields. At the visual energy level space did not separate. A deeper part of me, however, and something very much separate from any rational volition, lunged my body forward as though someone had bumped into me, as though someone or something energized me to extend my arm. Somewhat involuntarily, I outstretched my hand and pointed my index finger directly toward a man leaning against the wall in the back of the auditorium. Then I saw his entire luminous cocoon and a yellow ray like a giant ribbon pointing down behind his left shoulder. It was not my eyes that saw him first, however, at least not the forty percent. This man slowly worked his way through the crowd, limping toward the stage.

Dom Inacio again walked over to me and leaned his shoulder against mine and whispered, "He just had a car accident and his back is broken. Now I want you to heal him."

The man now stood directly in front of me. A large-framed, physically powerful man in his early thirties, he looked me squarely in the eyes and held my gaze without a blink. No doubt he saw my trance eyes become too normal as my forty percent mind overran my thoughts.

Broken back? Heal him? thoughts about vertebrae started to materialize in my mind until I commanded it to silence.

Back and forth I went from thoughts to silence while this man stood there, obviously in pain, waiting, waiting for me to do something. The minutes went by as we stood there simply looking deeply into each other's eyes. With each burst into my silence from a mind wanting to know what to do, an unbearable tension pushed in my temples. Gurgling up from my unconscious I remembered my promise to don Eduardo to never fully incorporate a spirit and in that moment I wondered if I had made a mistake? In that moment I saw and understood not only the gift, but also the practical wisdom of the fully incorporated medium. *Who would want to put themselves through this!* My mind, my personal *idEntity*, required such enormous concentration to control that if I knew how to incorporate, in that moment I would have gladly given over to a spirit to heal this man. What could "I" do, after all, with a thousand people watching?

Suddenly this man broke eye contact and looked haplessly at Dom Inacio. "He can't do anything," he complained to the Entity and stepped back to rest his hands on his knees to ease his pain.

That moment could have been humiliating but instead I felt compassion for this man, realizing this was as difficult for him as it was for me. He required as much faith as I did, perhaps more, although we were attempting to move beyond faith. I would have gladly healed him if I could but I did not know what to do in these circumstances except to look into his eyes and see him as clearly as I could.

Finally Dom Inacio walked over to me, took my hand and placed it on his hip. In that moment something clicked, I knew what to do, what the Entity meant. My face softened and I looked deeply into this man's eyes with only love and appreciation for him while I firmly placed both of my hands on both of his hips. His eyes returned to me a very kind look as the energy began to vibrate in me. First it came in gentle ripples and then it escalated with enough intensity that we both held each other very tightly so as not to break apart. Intense tremors increasingly shook from deep within me and imparted a vibration into this man until we both held each other like wrestlers in a standing embrace. The energy was so strongly palpable that we could have been standing on some kind of vibrating machine that required our mutual support so as not to fall over. And then it stopped. I stepped back and Dom Inacio told the man to bend over and touch his toes a few times and to run up and down the ramp to the stage. Smiling broadly, the man reported his pain was entirely gone and Dom Inacio said his back would bother him no longer.

Feeling very detached as I watched the man's actions still I shared the gratitude he expressed to Dom Inacio. I also felt relieved that my part was now complete without considering what that had been. I was still deep in trance even though I was aware of everyone nearby and somewhat aware of the audience. I started to walk off the stage.

"Not so fast," Dom Inacio said, taking my shoulder and holding me steady with a kind and firm grip. He motioned toward a mother holding her little boy by the shoulders, a child who shook spastically with involuntary twitches and strange grimaces that frequently jerked his entire body.

"Mother, bring your son here," Dom Inacio said, looking squarely at the woman, who gasped with gratitude when Dom Inacio pointed to her. Holding this wriggling child was no small feat, yet she firmly and with great care helped her twitching son onto the stage.

"Now heal him," Dom Inacio said to me a little dramatically. "He needs your help now."

This time my mind remained quiet and the forty-percent was calm. There was such absolute authority and conviction in Dom Inacio's command that it took "me" completely out of the picture. I looked at this mother as she escorted her little boy into my hands; he writhed and twisted as I attempted to hold him. An outpouring of love filled me. I inwardly said to God that I knew I could do nothing here but I would be a vehicle for His Love. I kneeled down and placed my palms on both sides of this little boy's temples. Fully covering the sides of his little face with a very firm grip while wrapping him in my elbows I tried to hold him to my chest. He never did look at me. At first he thrashed violently but I did not let go while his body torqued and kicked until I trapped his legs with mine. Without hurting him I took great care not to allow his head to move. Finally there was a moment where I felt he accepted my grip and allowed his head to rest firmly between my hands. For a while he thrashed and writhed from below the neck until eventually, in maybe five or more minutes, he became completely calm. Once again an intense vibration shook through me and then it was done.

I stood up and noticed my doctor friend was still on the stage standing next to me. The little boy's mother burst into sobs and grabbed Dom Inacio, kissing his hand profusely while thanking him. When the entire session was over the mother came up and hugged me. I felt embarrassed and not responsible but I accepted her gratitude with more gratitude than I knew how to express to her. Her son had sat quietly through the entire afternoon session, she told me, and he had never been still for five minutes since he was born. I looked down at him fussing next to her like any normal five year old and when he reached out and grabbed my pant legs for a moment, I wanted to kneel and convey something I could not easily understand myself. Instead I gave them both a hug.

Characteristic of the Entity's healing, there was no self-congratulation. Dom Inacio immediately called another person onto the stage and performed a physical, cutting on the flesh, operation and then requested that my doctor friend suture him. Dom Inacio said this man had had a blocked heart valve and he had corrected it. I learned later that the straight needle and Dom Inacio's instructions belonged more to a turn-of-the-last-century operational style. My friend was used to different needles. Although the patient never reacted with pain or bleeding, sewing him up with a thousand people watching was not the easiest task.

Suddenly Dom Inacio staggered slightly and looked like he might collapse. He walked over to me and firmly took my hand and then the doctor's and whispered to us, "The medium is very tired. His body does not easily hold my energy." Dom Inacio fiercely grabbed our hands and leaned on us for full support to remain erect.

When Dom Inacio took my palm and his weight literally dropped onto me, I realized Joao the Medium needed *current* and Dom Inacio was asking something of me. I had more than enough strength to carry the medium in my arms like a child if need be, even though he was a large man and I am not, but he needed something more than simply being held, he needed to be fed an energetic jumpstart. The shamans of Peru had taught me very well. I understood exactly what he wanted from me. I opened my palm chakra, the same hand he had pierced, and I willingly gave him open access to my energy field. His left hand leaned into my right palm as if he were using my hand for a cane to lock onto a current. I cupped him from behind, holding his left side while my doctor friend held his other side. We walked off the little stage and through the door, maintaining this mutual grip.

When the Entity leaves the stage it means the public surgery and healing is over. The Entity leaves the stage and goes to the Entity Room where he most often sits in a chair and receives each person, one by one, and gives personal attention to every person in line until it is done. On days like this with a large crowd, that can take a while although the line moves surprisingly quickly. Half carrying him, we walked Dom Inacio back to the Entity Room and sat him in his chair. Almost as soon as he sat down a younger, almost lithe and limber animation took over Joao's body.

"Dom Inacio thanks you," the Entity said with a crisper, almost cheery voice.

It was not Dom Inacio who was now speaking to us, but most likely one of the medical doctor entities. Joao's hair had become scraggly and the Entity fished the medium's glasses from his pocket and put them on. Some of the turn-of-the-century doctor entities like the glasses but most never use them. Another Entity had entered the medium's body and was able to maneuver in Joao's frame with a great deal more strength. For the rest of the session sometimes it would be Dom Inacio sitting there, and other times one of the doctor entities. Only the senior mediums in the room, authorized to have their eyes open during session, would have likely noticed, especially when the line was moving quickly.

We witnessed one more mind-blowing healing miracle before the day ended. It was late in the afternoon and one of the longest sessions I had ever attended. The setting sun was shooting parallel shafts of light across the top of the room through high windows along the wall. I noticed the light in the room changed from reddish-orange sunset colors to a soft golden hue. The already peaceful, utterly holy feeling enveloping the room intensified and made my chest feel like a radiant hole of loving energy.

After receiving a number of people fairly quickly, giving them a prescription for a spiritual herbal remedy, or an instruction to return another day, the line had been moving fairly quickly with no prolonged attention toward anyone. Suddenly, the Medium stood up from his chair with a strong and profound presence and asked everyone in the room to open their eyes. It is a cardinal rule when sitting in the presence of the Entity, that the audience "must" keep their eyes closed so the invisible entities performing healing can be effective. The Entity requires most people when *sitting in his current rooms* or meditating in his sessions to keep their eyes closed unless they are standing in line waiting their turn to face him directly. Entity does authorize some people to have their eyes open continuously during sessions in the *current rooms*, such as senior mediums there to assist, or other special cases such as a film crew. Failing to keep your eyes closed will compromise results and your permission to attend the sessions. Occasionally Entity will tell people in the room to open their eyes so they may watch something he is doing, such as this moment, and would only do so if enough of a unified field of love-based attention was present throughout the room.

It was Dom Inacio before us again. He looked directly at the next person in line: a Brazilian woman in her early thirties dressed in ordinary street clothes. The Entity walked up to her and brought his face to within a few inches of hers. She gasped, clasping her hands to her chest, and reacted as though the most wonderful and tender news imaginable had just arrived though *neither of them had spoken a word.*

"What would you do if God healed you?" Dom Inacio firmly asked with the warmest friendliness.

Almost falling down in a swoon, her answer was clear enough. Dom Inacio placed his hands on both of her shoulders standing alongside her like a coach, or her father. Then with both hands he brusquely and suddenly reached down and pulled up her blouse, exposing her bare chest, and when he did so his hands accidentally tapped her chin, which sent her into a trance. Her head fell slightly backwards and her eyes remained closed and with Dom Inacio holding her she remained steady and erect. The woman's right breast was full, healthy appearing and normal, but her left breast was blackish-brown and gray, distorted and distended; obviously something was very wrong.

"Medicos, medicos, please, would the doctors in the room come forward," Dom Inacio requested.

I noticed my friend was so deeply entranced watching that he did not realize he was being called. I nudged him with my elbow.

"Please, would the doctors in the house come forward," Dom Inacio asked once again.

My friend and another woman, a doctor from South Africa, approached the afflicted woman, whose head had fallen backward because of her deep trance. Dom Inacio stood behind her while holding her firmly by the shoulders.

"Please, examine her breasts and tell us what is there," Dom Inacio requested.

Both doctors examined her breasts and reported that one appeared healthy and normal and the other was hard and completely necrotic.

Dom Inacio moved in front of the woman and held her face in his hands and gently said, "God loves you."

Without any forewarning Dom Inacio swiftly turned and grabbed me where I was standing a few feet away. With surprising strength and dexterity he quickly turned me around and bent me forward by the neck. Then he leaned the woman backwards onto my back, aligning our spines, while I reached back and held her. Exhaling deeply, Dom Inacio firmly pushed his hand across her throat and down across her necrotic breast as though he was pushing a great weight off of her chest. He repeated this movement several times, exhaling dramatically with a final flourish and enough pressure that I could feel the weight of his push. I then lifted her from my back by gently standing up straight. Dom Inacio stood behind her and placed his hands on her shoulders like a proud father presenting her breasts to the room. Many people burst out crying and murmurs and prayers filled the room while my own eyes teared up. The woman standing before us now had two lovely breasts.

"Medicos, please, would the doctors come forward and tell us what is there," he requested.

Once again the doctors walked up and carefully examined the woman's breasts. The female doctor was so moved that she continually held and embraced the Brazilian lady until they were both smiling and in tears. My friend tried to be a great deal more professional with his palpations and such, but he also looked a little dazed with disbelief. At the Entity's request, the doctors gave us their report but they could tell us nothing our own eyes had not already confirmed. Both her breasts were perfectly normal.

I have been present at more than a few extraordinary events in my life and this was one of those times that legitimately falls into the category of miracle. A loving presence filled my heart and every person's heart in that room. Moments later, Dom Inacio turned to the next person in line with no self-congratulations of any sort, as though nothing out of the ordinary had occurred. Each remaining person in line received Dom Inacio's full and undivided attention for whatever was needed.

As it turned out, my rapture was short-lived although I will never forget that miraculous afternoon. Walking out of the *current* (energy) room soon after the session had ended, difficult feelings began welling up in me. *What was it that had happened to me this day and what was I supposed to do with it?*

I was not experiencing trivial head chatter; it was deep and sober reflection. I felt very awake and alive, expanded even, but also thrown into territory that demanded I account to myself for my own experience. I sat down on a concrete bench along a wall toward the back of the Casa where it looked out on a garden spot said by the mediums of the house to be a portal to other dimensions. While I was sitting there, the mother and her little boy I had helped heal approached me calmly. They were holding hands and looking like any normal, healthy mother and child; the boy was lively though his twitch was gone. Dressed in street clothes, they had arrived that day on one of the large buses chartered from a distant city. One to ten buses can arrive for any session, sometimes leaving the same day; sometimes people slept on the bus, other times they stayed in the many little motels near the Casa. The courage, willingness, and faith required on their part to make this enormous change almost brought me to tears! Yes, it was certainly Dom Inacio's *current,* the term for the Entity energy at the Casa, and ultimately God who delivered them, and yes, I had done my part, but I knew all too well that healing must also be their choice as well. It's a decision one must make and whether it's with God and/or your own inner world, it's still a decision and a choice. I was simply in awe at their gentle innocence and in truth I could have gotten on my knees and kissed their shoes for the spiritual demonstration they placed in front of me.

As they walked away a raw, in my gut, feeling began to stew. I knew what it was and had felt it many times along the way, though never with such point-blank clarity. I felt unworthy, inauthentic, and very uncomfortable, at least "it" did, and those feelings produced another mental wrestling match. I knew this feeling was my *false idEntity*, the very problem it proclaimed to resist. False mind chatter *idEntity* that took credit and made complaint but in fact had no real validity whatsoever. If you know your own mind, then you understand me because I'm talking about something entirely universal as well as my own process. Recognizing my egotistical thoughts did not automatically stop the feelings.

Whatever healing or positive outcome had taken place this day, I did not feel worthy of accepting any credit, yet I recognized something in me had played a part. I had kept my promise to Shaman don Eduardo Calderon, although also realizing I had not understood at the time the consequences of my choice and the same was likely true of today. What this day would mean in my life, I would have no way of knowing for a long while. I could not accept any self-congratulatory feelings, especially when by example I had seen Dom Inacio accept none, but neither did I need to accept self-judging thoughts or feelings. For the first time I understood why so many monks take up a single-room existence of abstinence and celibacy. How does one forgive oneself for a life of arrogance even when you realize you simply knew to be no different? The very last thing I would have ever selected for myself was to stand in front of the Casa of Dom Inacio and claim to heal anyone. Yet there I was. It happened and now something in me felt like an imposter or wanted to feel special and a deeper part of me did not identify with either. Even though I understood the inner landscape playing in my mind, it was still demanding to navigate.

Now the shaman's promise took on its full implications while the whole realization flooded my being; what I now understood was don Eduardo's point. The shaman demands that the *impersonal* manifestation of the spirit called *"power"* work through him in a way that he has some say so. It's a personal predilection: the way the shaman retains a healthy identity and can understand himself distinct from what moves through him. However humbly or arrogantly, the shaman interacts with something he acknowledges to be greater than himself and of which he is also a part. He seeks to be acted upon by *spiritual power* and to be allowed some say about the outcome. The medium, on the other hand, may never understand his part *except to give himself over entirely to an individual spirit with superior abilities,* at least in Medium Joao's case, *while relinquishing all personal consciousness and all personal responsibility.* Both act as vehicles and both credit The Spirit as the cause and source, except the medium personalizes it to fully sentient beings such as Dom Inacio. The shaman, on the other hand, beckons The Spirit by entering the *nagual* and retains enough *self-idEntity* to credit the impersonal manifestation *power* for whatever occurs. Retaining that recognition remains important to the shaman for whatever reason. The *idEntity* and self-perceived function are different, although I am fairly certain that both The Shaman and Medium Joao say exactly the same thing in the end. *Let the one who can act do so.*

I still had plenty of good reasons why I would not willingly give myself over in mediumship and the service of healing others, although this day had changed the attraction of the goal. It had become entirely purified and was now seen clearly by me as a holy assignment for those who can fulfill it. I asked myself: Would I be willing to totally let go, to completely relinquish my time/space existence *idEntity* and trust that it would be returned to me in a safe condition? Medium Joao once told me that Dom Inacio protects and takes charge whenever he incorporates and no unwanted spirits can attach to him. What about the rest of us? How does one strike up a relationship with a protective Entity with enough authority to do that? Trust in God, Medium Joao would tell me, but I did not feel he answered my question. That part was a given but what about the internal moves on the way in and out of the incorporated state? After all, the medium is performing something unique and demanding.

Don Eduardo insisted the shamans say: Don't fully incorporate; stand there on your own two feet, face to face with the spirit and interact as equals. Well, the first part I had certainly done this day. I did stand there on my own two feet, face-to-face, but not the second. Equals? My experience that afternoon told me that only arrogance would make such a claim. I did not feel equal to Medium Joao or Dom Inacio, far from it, but neither did I feel inferior. Standing in the light of both spiritual masters was glorious and hellish. I was not comparing personalities or feeling sorry for myself, simply being honest as best I could. I knew at a level of truth that we were equal parts of the same whole, but on this plane I was not equal to their ability to act. I was, however, no longer certain which choice was wisdom: the shaman's or the medium's? Not to give over entirely to an incorporated spirit looked like an inadequate choice in the light of the healing that occurs at the Casa of Dom Inacio through Medium Joao Teixeiria de Faria.

An Entity once explained to me through Medium Joao that it is easier for him (than presumably you or me) to manifest The Spirit's healing because he is no longer attached to a human *idEntity* living in a body to distract his mind. I understood his point exactly except I almost choked when I heard him say that, because he was obviously looking at me through the eyes of a body *that he required*. How could I not observe the obvious contradiction? The Entity immediately read my thoughts and dryly replied that I was mistaken, that he did not require the medium's body to heal anyone, rather I did in order to believe.

Epilogue

As of this writing it's been three and a half years since that day with Dom Inacio at his Casa in Abadiania. Since that day I have never again seen Dom Inacio incorporated in Medium Joao nor have I ever been called to "hands on" heal anyone and I'm grateful for that. There are so many gifted, sincere and quality healers in the world who can fix the body through spiritual and energetic means that I am certain they are given the assignment and perform it very well. Look around; they are there, many who offer alternative medicine and others who offer healing energy work and many offer both. It does not require a person with Medium Joao's staggering gifts to heal you. In my experience there are many practitioners who can heal IF AND WHEN you are ready to make the necessary mental, emotional and attitudinal changes necessary to stabilize what the healer can offer you.

The Spirit does knock on my door quite regularly and I daily enjoy the process. My original request that day to The Entity Dom Inacio continues to be answered as I learn to direct spiritual energy into all of my desires and needs while I learn from The Spirit what they are. This precise lesson I benefit from on a daily basis, the very same lesson of both the shaman and the medium. I have learned to listen and to pay attention on many levels: to omens, to feelings of all kinds, to communication that speaks to me in many ways, and I recognize I am never alone. Not intellectually recognize, that I did a long time ago. I mean something that is stable and constant and real within my ongoing experience. To say I recognize I am never alone sounds so simple and almost trite. Yet entering into that full realization presents a level of visceral impact; Carlos Castaneda once told me personally that it almost killed him. I share the sentiment; the impact is huge. He meant finally remaining awake, all the time, in the full realization and participation that your personal consciousness is not private and never has been. That includes your bathroom habits and every thought you've had but never remember.

Everything: personal feelings, awareness, consciousness AND unconsciousness, including specific thoughts, all exist on LOUDSPEAKER and on BULLETIN BOARD to many levels of consciousness and life form. In fact, in all of the universes we two-leggeds are the only ones confused about that and our relentless pretense, on a grand scale called humanity, in no way changes the reality of shared consciousness. Shamans, Spirits and Mediums serve us with their sacred reminder that we share levels of being, consciousness and existence that are before and after this material world we inhabit within a body and a lifetime. No matter how convincing the appearances of death, neither the body nor its lifetime are final. We do not begin or end with either.

There's a great deal more that can be intelligently discussed and asserted about what it all means and I am grateful to others who contribute to our understanding. As to the larger discussion of who and what are spiritualist mediums and shamans such as Joao de Deus and don Eduardo Calderone, I have preferred to share my own experiences more than my opinions. That was certainly the guidance of both these masters, to trust in your own experience and let it reveal your truth.

I can corroborate and personally verify the absolute and undeniable reality of coherent and self-referential awareness beyond the body within compassionate conditions of existence and operating under a Senior Authority of Love. I believe I have accomplished such a personal verification, at least that's the paradigm of reality that has taken shape for me from these experiences I have related. I know that my own life, including my personal consciousness, does not begin or end with this life or body. Each of us is an immortal entity. There have always been those among us who exist to demonstrate we are spirits inhabiting bodies, and their demonstrations nourish our sense of being safe and loved within something greater than our understanding. Since the beginning, means have been given to many kinds of people to venture beyond ideas and belief systems to seek direct contact and personal experience with transpersonal reality. My tales have revealed some of the means given to me and perhaps the telling will offer something for my readers.

To make what I have seen of the sacred living embodiment of the shaman and the medium as real as possible, I have shared personal and precious experiences in this book with the intention of being as real with you as the topic allows. What do these experiences affirm for me, you may ask? Well, just this exactly as I said above. *I know it to be true within my being that I am a fully intact, coherent and self-referential consciousness existing within peaceful and loving conditions of self-awareness independent of the body.* Living with this understanding is a new beginning, a way of living my own existence as well as creating authentic relationships with others.

There is only one ultimate journey and we all share the same path. Not the journey to the grave, a shallow marker of what cannot be final, but the journey of awakening. We are more, much more than we culturally sanction ourselves to see and understand unless we choose to see and understand ourselves more directly and therefore honestly. Were it not for shamans and spiritualist mediums of all kinds in the multifaceted threads of humanity, as well as The Spirit that illumines them, we would be in danger of forgetting. Our collective dream is just that, a stop on the way Home, a cosmic motel to hang out in for a few lifetimes. Shamans, spirits and mediums show us that we are alive forever and ONLY LOVE IS IN CHARGE. Orient your compass only to that bearing and you will walk an ancient path called by many names that always leads Home.

To purchase this book directly from the author:

800 phone#: 1-(888) 844-4739

URL address: www.highholyadventure. com

Printed in the United States
22653LVS00001B/206